THE GREEN SILK DRESS

by

Marie Cross

Marie Cross

17. 7. 10

Dedicated to the memory of those who were drowned
in the Hartlake tragedy 1853
and to my son, Simon, who had a social conscience.

AUTHOR'S NOTES

This is a novel. However, I have incorporated within it a true event, which took place in 1853. This has necessitated introducing people who lived at that time, about whose private lives I know little.

John and Jane Eldon, for example, had three children whom I have completely ignored for the purpose of the story and, as the Eldons play a major part in the novel, I have had to give them characters. The Bell was enlarged in the middle of the nineteenth century though I do not know exactly when so, as John Eldon was also a builder, I have made him the one who carried it out.

The gypsies have been given characters. They cannot be found in the census as I understand itinerant persons were not included. Descendants of these gypsies are still alive and there is a letter from the great, great, great granddaughter of Emily Taylor (who survived the tragedy) in the archives in Tonbridge Library. I have found, from the 1851 census, the names and occupations of some minor characters who lived in Golden Green or Tonbridge.

The account of the inquest is adapted from the Kentish and South Eastern Advertiser of the time. The jurors, who were mainly tenant farmers, and the coroner, are real people, as were the two representatives of the Medway Navigation Company and the Registrar.

There is a story in the archives of a boy sitting on his mother's coffin. I have given the boy the name of Patrick and made Catherine Clare his mother. This is a figment of my imagination.

The blacksmith in Golden Green was called Vanns and a family of that name still live there, and I have been told they have no objection to my using that name for my fictitious family.

I trust that any inaccuracies will be forgiven by those who have a connection with the real persons in the story.

ACKNOWLEDGEMENTS

My thanks to Mrs Anne Hughes of the Hadlow Historical Society and an authority on the disaster. She kindly provided me with information, showed me around St Mary's Church in Hadlow and read through my manuscript.

Mr Stewart Main, Master Brewer at Shepherd Neame, for his assistance with brewing processes.

Dr John Ray and Eileen Best for checking my manuscript.

Mrs Mary Horner (her father was a Hern) for help with Romany phrases.

Emily Featherstone who gave me pointers on learning to ride a horse.

Martin Publishing
35 Exeter Close
TONBRIDGE, Kent
TN10 4NT
United Kingdom
Tel: 01732 350670

ISBN   0-9546146-2-3

Cover design by Jean Hill
Printed and bound by CPI Antony Rowe, Eastbourne

CHAPTER 1

September 1851

Richard Wakefield alighted at Tunbridge Station. The top-hatted stationmaster sternly eyed his staff as porters took leather suitcases and bags from the better-dressed, first class passengers and loaded them on to trolleys to take to waiting carriages. Doors slammed, the squat engine belched smoke, steam hissed and a whistle shrieked. Richard contemplated asking the stationmaster how to get to Golden Green, but he struck him as being too important, so he followed the crowd out of the station. He assumed from the appearance of a few of them that they had come for the hop picking just as he had, though it was late in the season. He turned to a man close by.

'Could you tell me the way to Golden Green, I've been...?'

'Left outta station, turn right into main street, go over the bridges and turn right afore Rose & Crown.' Before he could thank him, he was gone.

Richard followed the fast dispersing crowd in the general direction specified by the man. As he came to the main street his nostrils were immediately assailed by the foulest of smells. Was there a meat market nearby? He could only equate the odours with those that emanated from the meat and fish markets he had been to in London. The ill-paved roads of the main street were wet and muddy, and intermittently clapperboards covered the streams that crossed the street, the bridges seemingly inadequate for the task. He passed beer houses where rowdy crowds of men were spilling out on to the road, some laughing inanely, others spoiling for a fight. He peered down alleys where cottages, for want of a better description, had ragged, shoeless children playing in the filthy yards. Houses and shops, interspersed with fields, skirted each side of the street. The heavy clouds darkened the sky but he estimated the time to be only around three o'clock.

After several streams he could still see no turning through the drizzle that had just started. He turned up his coat collar and took his leather cap from his pocket. To the left a castle loomed through the rain as he reached a more imposing bridge with wharves and boats being loaded and unloaded. If the weather had been more clement he would have stayed to watch, always curious to gain new knowledge and experiences.

Further on the area appeared smarter and the smell less offensive. It began to rain harder as Richard asked a passer-by how far to the turning for Golden Green.

'Near Rose & Crown up there,' he pointed a finger, 'turn right 'long Swan Street then you'll see a signpost for Hadlow. Follow that.'

'How far is it to Golden ...?' But he, too, had gone.

Soon after leaving Swan Street he passed a toll where a cart was waiting to pay. Miserably he walked on, hoping to see a fingerpost saying Golden Green. He became more and more despondent and wished he had stayed at home in Clapham. After what seemed hours of tramping almost ankle deep in mud, he saw the welcome sign. Just to make sure, he shouted to a passing waggoner to ask if the Bell Inn was far down the road.

'Not far, just over a mile. I would give you a lift, but I have to go into Hadlow before I come back to Golden Green.'

Richard was tempted to ask if he could go into Hadlow with him - anything to get out of the mud and wet - but he had no idea if Hadlow were close or miles and miles away.

Richard staggered into the stabling yard of the Bell and wearily rested his tall frame against the front door before pushing it open and walking into a narrow passage. He almost fell into the taproom. Through its warm smoky atmosphere a few country labourers turned to look at him, then returned to their ale and pipes. He pulled off his cap.

'Got caught in the rain, eh?' the landlord said as he approached the counter. 'What can I get you? You look as if you could do with drying off those clothes.' He shouted across to the men sitting on a bench near the fire. 'Hey, make room for this young lad. He's dreaning wet.' He turned back to Richard. 'I'll bring your drink over to you, pint of our local brew?'

Richard nodded, and gratefully did as he was told. He stood close to the fire and although the apple logs were spitting dangerously, he was too tired to care, warmth was all he desired at that moment.

'You come for the 'opping den?' someone asked. 'You're a bit late.'

'Yes.'

'Almost finished now, just a few drifts of the early crop, den de late one.'

'You're beginning to steam,' another man said, and they all laughed. Richard managed a weak smile.

'S'rained a lot lately – ground's sodden. Won't be much fun picking hops in de rain,' an old man remarked gloomily.

'No,' Richard agreed. He had only a vague idea what hopping entailed, with or without rain, and most of that he had gleaned from a man he had met on the train who was going on to Wateringbury. It was only on the spur of the moment he had decided to see what hop picking was all about.

'Here, come and sit down. My name's Robert.' The man, in his thirties, shifted along the bench to make room. 'You oughter get out of those clothes directly. Got anywhere to stay?'

'No, not yet. Someone on the train suggested I walk to this inn, but I had no idea it was so far from the station. I'm not used to walking this far.'

'One of dese softie Lunnuners, eh?' suggested a bewhiskered man, wearing a calico smock. He waved his clay pipe at him.

Richard gave a wan smile and began to shiver. 'Do you think I could stay here? Have they lodging rooms?' he asked Robert, dreading the answer might be no.

'They might.' Robert shouted to the landlord, 'You got a vacant room for this lad, John?'

The innkeeper held up his finger and disappeared, returning a moment later. 'Yes, but you'll have to wait a while until the girl's made up a bed.'

'There, you'll soon feel better. Where're you going to pick?'

'The man on the train said to ask for a Mr Cox; said he'd got a good reputation. Is his place near here?' Richard could not bear the thought he still had to walk miles to a hop field. It seemed to him that there were nothing but hop fields on his walk from the station.

'Yeah. Thompson's, down the lane. Farms a tidy few acres round here.'

'Is he good to work for, like the man said?' Though he had asked the question, Richard could not have cared less if he were or not, it was the thought of a bed and relief from his cold, sodden clothes that loomed large, but he did not like to be rude.

'As good as most farmers round here,' replied Robert. 'You does the work, you gets paid the going rate which isn't a lot. I'll take you to see him in the morning if you like. Sometimes he gets overwhelmed with pickers, but one extra won't make much difference. He says he'll soon have to say who he wants in the future and not just have hoards of Londoners descending on him. The railway coming in forty-two made a difference. Before that, those from London all walked down here and that kept the numbers lower. Most still do – can't afford the fare, see, especially if they've a big family.'

Richard gratefully sipped his drink until the landlord called, 'Right young man. Room's ready. Follow me.'

They climbed the bare wooden stairs to a door at the top of the staircase, which opened to reveal a square, sparsely furnished room at the back of the building though it looked on to the road. It had plain walls with a picture of a rural scene on one of them.

'Trust this will be satisfactory for tonight. If you're staying longer, the girl will get the fire going tomorrow. Goodnight. '

Richard peered through the window, across the road, and on to the fields. He could not see clearly because of the pelting rain, but in the gloom of dusk he noticed a weird shaped building with a pointed roof like a squat spire and something white on the top that moved with the wind. The September light was fading fast and he pulled the heavy curtains, lit the candle on the table beside the bed and took it over to the washstand. He removed his wet jacket, neckerchief, waistcoat and trousers. He could not see how they would be anywhere near dry by the morning without a fire. He poured cold water from a large blue and white earthenware jug into a matching bowl and washed his hands and face, shivering in the cold air. Taking off his undergarments, he lay under the counterpane and stared at the ceiling. For the second time he wondered what he was doing in Kent? What on earth had brought him to this place? He had no connections here; knew absolutely nothing about the country in general and hop picking in particular. He supposed it was something his brother had said before he died that made him contemplate this last minute journey.

"'Look, Richard. I'm not going to live much longer ...'
'Don't say that, Chris, please. How will I cope without you?'
Chris put up his hand. 'Richard, I have consumption, you know that. I want you to do something with your life, not just stay around in London working in an office. Go round this country, then see the world if you've a mind to. I've saved a little money and you'll have the house. You'll manage, I know it.' He squeezed Richard's arm."

Richard's eyes began to fill. His brother had always looked after him when first their father, then two years later their mother had died. Christopher, ten years older, did not send him out to work as other lads younger than his twelve years would have been, but let him stay on at a school so he could continue his education and not stop at just learning to read and write. Christopher had served his apprenticeship as a cabinetmaker and had only been working for a few years when his health began to fail and he had to leave.

Richard started as he heard a knock on the door and a head peered round.

'I thought you might like to have your clothes dried. When we've shut, Grace can keep the fire going.' The landlord looked about him and saw the clothes spread out on the chair and the rails of the bed. Realising Richard had no clothes on, he said, 'I'll take them all if that's all right with you. I'll bring them back in the morning.' He began gathering up the jacket and trousers. 'Do you want something to eat? We've bread and some cheese or ham. I've no doubt the wife can cook you something.'

'No, no thank you. I'm not hungry.'

'Very well.' He moved towards the door. 'You've come for the hop picking?'

'I thought I'd see what it's like. Sounds interesting.'

'Don't know about interesting – hard work more like, especially if you're not used to it.' He grinned, as he opened the door. 'Don't know your name young man, what is it?'

'Wakefield. Richard Wakefield.'

'My name's John Eldon. We'll see you in the morning then. The girl'll light a fire in here if you're staying. Goodnight.'

Funny he was not hungry, Richard thought, as the landlord shut the door. He had hardly eaten all day. He started thinking about his brother again but weariness overcame him and he slipped between the coarse sheets and fell into a deep sleep.

Richard opened his eyes and stared about the unfamiliar room. He caught sight of the rush chair beside the washstand where his clothes lay in a neat pile. He washed and put on his flannel vest and long pants. He picked up his shirt and slipped it over his head. It was creased but the creases had been smoothed out, likewise his trousers. He wondered what the time was. He drew back the curtains, staring at the unusual building in the distance. By the position of the bright sun, he thought it must be around mid morning. There was a tap on the door and Richard went to open it.

'Ah, I thought you must be awake,' John Eldon said, 'as me and the wife heard movements. Clothes all right, young man?'

'They certainly are.' Richard opened the door wider. 'Come in while I finish dressing, Mr Eldon.'

'The wife wanted to know if you would like some hot water but I see you've already washed. Can we get you something to eat?'

'Yes please, I'm famished. I should have taken up your offer of food last night, but I suppose I was just too tired and past it.'

'Right. I'll get Jane to get you some bacon and eggs. Bacon from our own pigs and eggs from our chickens. Ale to drink?'

'That'll be fine. I'll be down in a minute. You must let me know what I owe you.'

While he was eating, Robert Mills came in. 'I called earlier but John said you were still asleep. I've come to take you to see Mr Cox.'

'Yes, he told me. I'm sorry, I was so exhausted I must have slept for....' He shook his head. 'I don't know, fourteen or fifteen hours.'

'Never mind. When you've finished we'll go and see him.'

About half an hour later they were walking along the road and down a lane almost opposite the inn. Robert chatted away telling him about the fruit and the hops that grew around the area.

'There's also cereals,' he went on, 'but there's not much grown close by the river, that's all marshy meadow. Gets flooded does the river. In fact, it's nearly up to the banks already.'

'What river?'

'Why the Medway, of course. You really don't know much about us, do you?'

'Afraid not. I have a lot to learn. I never knew that hops grew so tall,' he said, studying the poles and the dark green leaves winding up them and the lighter green hops hanging in loose bunches. He reached up and felt some, expecting the hops would be hard, like the pine cones they resembled, but to his surprise, they were soft.

Mr Cox was talking to his bailiff when they arrived, and when he had finished, Robert introduced him.

'So, you want to do some picking. You're welcome to join us. John Lawrence, my bailey here, will put you with someone who knows the ropes, the Leatherlands and Herns, or maybe the Taylors. They're all related though I've never worked out their exact relationship. We're awaiting the late crop. The main crop is all but over. Come back day after tomorrow.'

Richard wondered what he could do till then. Though he had enough money on him for board and lodging for a while, it would not last forever, and he did not know what he would earn picking hops. Not a lot from the sound of it.

'Who are the Leatherlands and Herns? Do they come from London?'

'They're gypsies,' Robert replied. 'They've been coming here for generations. They travel where the seasonal work is, but they might winter somewhere, probably in London or on common land, I'm not sure.'

5

Richard was alarmed. 'Gypsies!' he exclaimed. His knowledge of gypsies was very limited, but they had a bad reputation. They were considered to be thieves and ne'er-do-wells and he had heard they dealt in witchcraft.

Robert laughed when he saw his expression. 'You don't want to believe everything you've heard about them. They're no better or worse than anyone else. So they do a bit of poaching, but they've got to eat somehow. It's better than the putrid meat that's sold to the Londoners most times. Mr Cox thinks highly of them because they're very hardworking. They also know a lot about curing people of their ills - cuts, coughs, broken bones, that sort of thing. Very good with horses, too.'

'Yes, I see.' He was not convinced.

When he arrived back at the inn, there was a girl in the room sweeping the floor. She was thin, poorly dressed, her expression listless. She was around twelve, maybe younger. She started as she caught sight of him.

'Hello.' She looked behind her as if he were speaking to someone else. 'Have you got a name?' Richard asked, as she prepared to leave.

'Grace,' she muttered, and scuttled away.

Richard stared after her. Obviously not a relative of the Eldons - much too unkempt. No doubt he would learn about her as he had determined to stay at the Bell for two weeks at least. Today he needed to go into Tunbridge. He did not relish his walk but the day was bright, if not particularly warm. So despondent had he been yesterday as he walked through the town, that he had not taken in as much as he would have liked. All that had impressed him, apart from the unfriendliness of some of its inhabitants, was the stench. Some London odours were not pleasant, but this smell had been particularly obnoxious, and he hoped the rain might have cleared the air somewhat. He was about to leave when he heard Mrs Eldon in the kitchen.

'You can go into town this morning and get these things for me,' she was saying sharply. 'I want some thread and a length of calico to make you a dress. Didn't bring much with you, did you?' She caught sight of Richard as they came through. 'I was just sending the girl into Tunbridge, Mr Wakefield,' she said putting on a swift smile. 'Needs a new dress, she does. Can't have her looking like a scarecrow, can we?' She put some coins into Grace's dirty hand and pushed her towards the door into the stabling yard.

'I'll go with her,' he said, hurrying after her.

She turned down the Hartlake Road.

'I thought you were going into Tunbridge,' Richard said as he caught her up.

'Don't go dat way,' she waved her arm up Three Elm Lane. 'I goes across de fields. It's quicker.'

'Isn't it muddy?'

She shrugged. 'Road's not much better.'

He knew that from his own experience, but her shoes were barely adequate to walk on any surface. Over her long-sleeved ragged dress of brown, she wore a dirty, white apron, which covered the top of the dress and ended about four inches above the ankle-length hem. She had no coat only a shabby, wool shawl, and a dirty white cap with a short piece of material that covered the back of her neck.

'Haven't you anything warmer to wear?'

'No, dis all I brought with me. Dey burned de rest.'

Richard frowned and went to ask her more, but she had hastened ahead and turned on to a path with a hop field on one side and an apple orchard on the other. Grace moved with surprising speed and he hurried to keep up, making a note to stay close when they were in the town as he was certain he would have difficulty finding his way back - not by this route anyway.

Ahead, Richard saw a man relieving himself in the hedge and nearby a boy and a girl were playing. Their mother was sitting nursing a baby and beside her was a barrow containing sundry pots, pans, and all they needed before their walk back. Richard shuddered at the thought. Further on was another family with innumerable children. Though they all appeared half-starved, and inadequately clothed, they seemed to be enjoying themselves as they chased each other around the hop poles. Richard was going to ask them where in London they came from, but Grace was far ahead.

Eventually they came out on the road that went from Tunbridge into Maidstone. He vaguely recognised it from the evening before. His shoes were caked in mud and those of Grace could not be seen at all, as the mud covered her ankles and splattered the hem of her dress.

'I suppose those people back there have come for the hopping,' Richard said.

'Swarm all over de place. Some 'ave gone 'ome already 'cause most of de 'ops is over.'

'Hm, yes, I see. You don't seem pleased to have them here.'

'Dirty lot dey are.'

Richard grinned. They continued their progress along the road into Tunbridge, this time side by side, as there was a little more room. They only had to resort to single file if two carts passed.

'I come from just outside London?' Richard said.

'From Lunnun?' she exclaimed. 'I'd love to go to Lunnun. Me mother come from dere.'

'Where's your mother?'

'Dead. Died of de fever.'

'When was that?'

'Last year, I think. In de winter anyway.'

'And your father?'

'Don't wanna talk 'bout 'im.'

They turned into the main street passing pastry shops, a shoemaker, and a printer and thence to the Rose and Crown. Coaches were lined up outside, depositing their occupants while the ostlers took the horses round the back of the inn to change them for fresh ones. It was market day and stalls of every description were set up on each side of the narrow road. Bread and cakes, meat, vegetables, fish, material, clothes and trinkets were piled on their respective trestle tables. Sheep and pigs going from the cattle market flocked down the road over the bridge, or were shepherded northwards to farms on higher ground, 'pass where dem grand 'ouses are,' Grace informed him. Other cattle were just arriving, causing mayhem everywhere.

7

They found a stall with swathes of various materials hung over wooden rails - coarse cotton, calico and gaberdine for workmen's smocks, wool, muslin, taffeta and some silk, which the better-dressed ladies were touching with kid-gloved hands. Grace was viewed with disdain and given a wide berth.

'One day I'm going to have a dress made of silk,' Grace informed him. 'When I get to Lunnun.'

Richard was about to inform her that London was no more likely to provide her with silk than she would get here, but he did not want to spoil her dreams - they all needed dreams.

She bought what was required and Richard purchased a length of ribbon for a farthing, which he gave to Grace. Though she thanked him curtly, her usually dull eyes held a little sparkle.

'I shall put this in my box,' she whispered. He wished he could buy her some shoes, but he had to keep a close watch on his money for the future if, as his dear brother had urged him, he was going to travel further afield in the future. Perhaps in two weeks if he earned enough, he might buy something for her. He did not want to touch the money that Chris said was in the bank - that was for something special. He bought a couple of buns and he and Grace sat by the horse trough in front of The Chequers to eat them.

With a bit of persuasion on Richard's part they were able to get a lift on a cart that had stopped at the tollgate on the road to Hadlow. It was travelling towards Maidstone loaded with chestnut hop poles. He had learned from Grace that Hadlow was quite close to Golden Green and he wished he had known that yesterday, and then he could have asked the waggoner if he could join him until he arrived back in Golden Green. They jumped off at Three Elm Lane. On the way, Richard told Grace about his brother and that he had no parents.

That evening Richard joined the men round the fire in the taproom. They were all labourers in the area – two, he learned, were shepherds, one called Thomas Willett and the other Henry Large, both from Hartlake. Thomas Vanns, a few years younger than him, was apprenticed to his father the blacksmith, also called Thomas.

Jane Eldon had provided him with an evening meal of meat and fresh vegetables which, he was informed as before, were grown on their land behind the stables. Probably 'the girl' as Grace was mostly referred to by Mrs Eldon, had had to pick and prepare them. He had not seen her since their trip to Tunbridge that morning.

'This girl Grace that works here,' he asked Robert. 'She told me her mother died of the fever.'

'That's right. Cholera it was.'

Richard opened his eyes wide. 'Poor girl. What about her father?'

'He was a good-for-nothing layabout. What little money he did earn he spent on drink. Used to knock his wife about, Grace as well. Cleared off as soon as his wife became ill.'

Richard knew life was hard and many folk were paupers and lived on the parish, but he could never abide hearing about cruelty. Perhaps it was because he came from a loving home. His parents had always impressed upon him and Chris to be considerate towards everyone whatever their station in life.

Robert went on. 'When her mother died, John took pity on Grace and brought her to live here. Don't think Mrs Eldon was all that pleased, but she's got a good servant.'

'Does she get a wage?'

'She gets free board and lodging.'

'Yes, but....'

'Don't worry about it. She's better off here than if she was sent to the workhouse, or just turned out in the street to fend for herself.'

'Are they allowed to do that?'

'Whatever they can get away with. The parish vestry committee might have done something.'

'Yes, I see.'

'Where does she sleep?' Richard persisted.

'Look here, why are you so interested?' He smiled slyly. 'Not planning on ...'

'I'm not planning on anything,' he said, his face reddening. 'Just interested, that's all. I feel sorry for her.'

Robert quickly changed the subject. 'We start tomorrow. I'll take you down to the garden where the gypsies are and introduce you.'

CHAPTER 2

A horn went off startling Richard, and hundreds of men, women and children were suddenly at work. He had never seen so many people and stood amazed. They were in long rows, which Robert told him were called drifts. Most were standing, but some who were elderly were sitting on stools or boxes. In front of them were large canvas holders, into which the hops fell.

'See,' said Robert pointing, 'the pole puller, with that hop dog and knife, is getting down the poles and laying them across holders so that the hops are picked straight from them.' Richard watched as the curved tool with a serrated edge prised up the pole, then the bine was cut at the base and the pole rested across the canvas bin. The pickers near him, mostly women, were removing the hops with amazing dexterity, and dropping them into the container. Some children were playing, but most of them were working beside their parents.

'Right, let me take you to where you'll be picking.' He led him over to a group of about sixteen people. They all had thick, jet-black hair and the older women had dark complexions and deeply lined faces. But what struck Richard was the beauty of the younger ones.

'Hello Mr Leatherland,' Robert said. 'This young man here has come to learn about hop picking. His name's Richard Wakefield and he comes from the outskirts of London. Mr Cox said you would show him what to do.' He turned to Richard. 'This is Samuel, the head of the family tribe.'

Samuel, a swarthy-skinned man in his fifties, looked up at him and solemnly nodded his head. He was dressed in thick brown trousers, a dark shirt with a waistcoat, another short coat on top of that and a red kerchief at his throat.

'This is his wife, Charlotte,' Robert continued, pointing to a woman wearing a large black hat and a long black dress with a shawl round her shoulders, crossed and tucked into her belt. She also nodded her head but did not look up.

'And these are their five daughters.' Robert swept his hand along the row. 'You'll learn their names in due course. Lunia here is married and has a child, over there.' He pointed to a girl of around two years old, who was at the end of the canvas hop container near her mother. She was putting hops into an upturned umbrella because she could not reach the container.

10

'Where's John then, Lunia?' Robert asked as he moved towards her.

'Up around somewhere.'

'John Hern is her husband,' he explained. 'Now you stand here for a moment and watch what they do. I'll go and get a box 'cause I don't suppose you'll be able to stay on your feet for ten hours.' He laughed and the family all grinned.

Richard was motioned to stand beside Samuel and he watched astounded as the hops fell into the holder at phenomenal speed. After a while, Samuel said to him, 'Now you try.'

Sitting on the apple box provided he reached for the bine and began to pick very slowly. He glanced at Samuel's fingers, but they moved so speedily, he could not even see what fingers to use.

'Like this,' Samuel said. He pulled a bine towards him and, with thumb and middle finger, deftly pulled the hop, leaving the leaves on the bine. 'They don't like any leaves with the hops.' He gave the ghost of a smile.

Richard followed his instructions and after about an hour began to work up a rhythm, slow, but he was getting faster. By the time he broke off for something to eat, he was quite pleased with himself. He opened the cloth that was wrapped around some thick ham and bread Mrs Eldon had provided. He took from the bag an earthenware jug which he thought contained a cordial, but he was surprised to find it was porter. Better not drink too much of that Richard thought, or he would be even slower. He tried to strike up a conversation with the women, but they were reserved and he had the impression that Samuel did not like them being familiar with him. Lunia's little girl, who he learned was called Centine, had no such inhibition and she chatted away, though Richard had to admit he could not understand a word she was saying. That went for all the Leatherlands when they were speaking amongst themselves, for they had their own Roma language. He did learn the names of two more of Samuel's daughters, Comfort and Fanny. Richard thought Fanny the loveliest woman he had ever seen with her thick, long black hair and black eyes. From her ears hung long gold hoop earrings, and she had a smile that melted his heart.

It was some while before Richard was put with a bin of his own. It was six feet long and about two feet wide and stood on trestles. It would take a long time for him to fill that. The gypsies said he could share the money they earned when he was with them, but he declined saying he had appreciated their help and company and he could hardly have contributed much anyway. He also felt that they had accepted him and they spoke to him a little more, though they were still wary of this gorgio. He had discovered that was what a non-Romany was called.

Richard approached Mrs Eldon a few days after he had started his hop garden adventure, and asked if Grace could come along with him. Reluctantly she agreed. Grace's face showed little emotion but, again, Richard could see from her eyes that she was pleased. She seemed to be afraid of showing her feelings.

'Have you been picking before?' he asked as they walked to the garden.

''Course. How else d'yer think my mum and me lived? We had no money else. My father drank away anything he got.' She paused, and then went on, 'He used to come with us sometimes, so he had more to buy drink with. Me Mum had to hide some of the money so she could pay the rent and we'd have something to eat.'

Grace attacked the hops in the same manner as the Leatherlands had, and his container was quickly filling. 'You're not very quick?' Grace scornfully informed him. 'You'll hardly make any money at dis rate. When tallyman comes, we'll hardly 'ave a bushel by end of de day.'

A bushel was a basket that the tallyman filled from their holder, Richard learned. 'How much do we get for a bushel?' he asked.

'A penny three farthings I think last time I heard, but nothing if you don't get quicker.'

He grinned. 'I know. I'm not used to this sort of thing. I work in an accountant's office writing up ledgers, and things.'

'How much do you get for doing that?'

'Fifteen shillings a week.'

'Fifteen shillings, just for putting ink on paper,' she exclaimed.

'There's a bit more to it than that. I had to learn to read and write and do sums.'

'I know my letters,' Grace said proudly, then more seriously, 'but me Dad said learning wasn't going to do me no good and so I worked in de fields, and den when he cleared off every so often, we *had* to work.'

Richard was not sure whether to ask the next question. 'How long – how long was your mother ill?'

Without slowing the pace of picking, she said, 'two weeks. De fever takes you directly.' Richard saw her eyes fill with tears, and he reached out his hand and covered hers, but she snatched it away.

'Do you like living with the Eldons?'

'It's better than de workhouse. Sarah and Stephen that I knowd went into de workhouse 'bout three year ago; there was no one to look after dem, see, when deir mother died. At least I wasn't sent dere. Mr Eldon is kind, though I don't think Mrs Eldon likes me much.'

'I think it's just her way,' Richard said, not wanting to undermine Jane Eldon's authority. However, he did think that Mrs Eldon resented Grace even though she had an unpaid servant at her beck and call.

While this conversation was going on the puller put another pole near their container. 'Come on you two, you'll not make much money at this rate.'

Richard said, 'so she keeps telling me, but it's not Grace, it's me, I'm afraid.'

'I'll make him go faster, Mr Diplock.'

'You do that young lady. Why them Leatherlands over there make more than eight to nine shillings a day.'

He stared in disbelief but on reflection, there were a great many of them and they worked very hard. No wonder the poor Londoners came. It was a break from their dreary lives as well as giving them some money, even if, as Robert Mills suggested, they did drink most of it away in the Tudely, Tunbridge or Hadlow beer houses.

Richard's preconceptions of gypsies were also undergoing a change. They seemed no different from anyone else he knew and they certainly did not shirk their work. True they were not very communicative, at least, not to him. One day, when he knew them better, he would ask them what some of the Romany words meant. Gorgio was the only word he knew. Perhaps he could go to visit their camps. Grace said they travelled around the country as a tribe wherever there was work, as many as thirty or forty of them, all related. Everything they owned was with them on trailers and carts pulled by their own horses and donkeys, and they lived in tents. In winter, she said, when there was no work in the country they camped on common land, but she did not know what else they did then to earn money.

Richard had been in the hop garden for two weeks. Grace came with him some days and he gave her some of the money he had from the tallyman, which, because of his lack of speed, amounted to very little, a paltry ten shillings. As before, Grace said she would put the money in her box. What else was in the box he was tempted to ask, but he thought she rather liked her secret. He could not imagine she had much of value.

One day there was great excitement amongst the gypsies. Richard gathered it was something to do with a vehicle one of the tribe had acquired. When John Hern passed by one afternoon, he asked him what it was all about. John put down his baby daughter and said, as she ran off to her mother, 'one of the tribe has made a vardo, one that you can live in, instead of putting the tents on the trailers or on the ground.'

'A vardo? What's a vardo?'

'This type of vardo is a sort of waggon on wheels. Something like travelling showmen go around in.'

Richard nodded. 'Like a caravan?'

'Yes, I think that's what you call them. It looks – it looks – well it'll be better than a bender tent, especially in weather like this.' It had been raining on and off for several days and picking was not a pleasant task. 'Our tents over Tudely are waterlogged most of the time lately. We have to dry them out while the women get a meal going, so they'll be reasonably dry come night time.'

'Can't you move to higher ground?'

John laughed. 'What higher ground?'

Richard grinned. 'I suppose there isn't much in a river valley. But not everyone lives in the open do they?'

'Some of them do, but the Irish travellers and a few of the Londoners live in the sheds and barns, some of them in pigsties. Most farmers don't care what happens to them as long as they do the work, so they just sleep in the fields like cattle. Mr Cox employs quite a few home dwellers and most of his travelling pickers have somewhere reasonably dry.'

One evening Richard managed to get Grace on her own. She had been picking with him for ten hours and on her return still had to do work at the inn. It was gone nine o'clock and Richard had been out to the privy. Grace was crossing the yard to go to the bigger stable opposite the inn's front door.

'Grace,' he called. She turned, and then continued walking. 'Grace, wait a minute.' He caught up with her. 'Why are you always in such a hurry? Can't you stop

13

and talk for a while?'

'I'm going to bed. Mrs Eldon will want me up early as usual and I'm dog tired.'

'Do you sleep out here – not in the house?'

'In the house?' she exclaimed. 'Where in the house?'

'No, I suppose there's not much room. There will be when Mr Eldon has finished the extension on the road side.'

'I sleep in the loft above de stable.'

'Is that all right?'

She shrugged. 'It's warm – the horses, you see. A bit smelly at times. I've got blankets.'

'Can I have a look?'

Grace hesitated. Unsophisticated she might be, but some of the ways of the world, and of men in particular, were not unknown to her, though she had never quite gathered what in particular she was to be wary about. 'You go tell Mr Eldon first.'

With a grin from the publican and acute embarrassment from himself, Richard returned to the stable. The horses snorted at his intrusion.

'Up here,' Grace called.

He climbed the ladder and hoisted himself to sit on the straw-covered loft floor. On three sides, straw and hay were stacked up to the ceiling, but in one corner Grace had made herself an alcove and Richard had to admit it was rather cosy.

"Course, when dey take de straw, I have to make de place again. But I don't mind. No one bothers me here.'

Grace was wearing her new dress and a cleaner apron, though this was beginning to look dirty. Richard wondered if it would be washed. Her feet were bare and filthy, as was the rest of her. Her muddy shoes lay nearby.

'Don't you...?' Richard began.

'Don't I what?'

'I don't know what to say. I don't want to upset you.'

'No one else is bothered.'

'I was going to say ...,' he still couldn't bring himself to be so rude. Grace pouted and put her head to one side. 'I was going to say why – why don't you wash yourself more often?'

'Wash! Me Dad used to say you could wash yourself too much. Not that I took much notice of 'im.'

'You haven't answered my question. Doesn't Mrs Eldon make you wash?'

'She'd better not. She tried once but I yelled so much she gave up. Now she don't mention it.'

'But you'd look so much nicer. And your hair – I hardly know what colour it is?'

'You don't have to look at me.'

'That's not the point. Don't you want to look...?' He was going to say pretty, but thought this might be misconstrued as wanting her to look pretty for him. That was true, he admitted to himself, but his desire was also for her to appear nicer for her own sake.

She changed the subject. 'You're very tall,' she said.

'Yes, I know. I was several inches taller than my brother. I'm nearly six foot and I have not met anyone taller than me. I think my mother's father was a tall man, but I did not know him.'

'It makes you stand out in a crowd.'

'How old are you? ' he asked.

'Fourteen.'

'When's your birthday?'

'Can't justly say de date. Around Easter time.'

'But you must have a birth certificate.' Grace shrugged and Richard said, 'My birthday's in April. Why don't you share mine? It's the 20th.'

She pursed her lips, and then said, 'All right. How old are you?'

'I'm twenty-one.'

'You look older than that.'

'Do I?'' Richard was rather pleased as he always thought he appeared young for his age. He had grown a moustache after his eighteenth birthday, but his hair was fair and the sparse moustache had not been an improvement, so he had shaved it off.

'I'd better go now and let you get some sleep.' He scrambled up. 'Are you picking with me tomorrow?'

'No. Missus wants me to do work here.'

'All right. Good night.' Richard negotiated the wooden ladder and crossed the yard to the front door. Mr Eldon had told him he was embarking on an extension to the Bell on the road side so Richard supposed that what was now the front door would then become the back of the inn.

Having decided to stay in Kent when the picking had ceased, he had made his room more homely. The fire had helped and he had kept it going day and night with the logs and coal left by the grate. Some daisies and buttercups had mysteriously appeared in a cracked earthenware jar, and he thanked Mrs Eldon. However, it appeared it was not her and she suggested it was probably Grace. Strange girl. Subdued on the one hand, forthright on the other. It was as if she were anxious to do better things, yet resigned to the fact that she never would.

CHAPTER 3

It was now early October. The continuous rain had stopped at last and for a week there had been sunshine. Mr Cox's farm was one of the few that planted a late crop. Most of the London pickers had packed up and were walking home and even some of the gypsies had moved on. However, the Leatherlands and nearly all their tribe were still in the area. Richard had speeded up his picking and was averaging six shillings a week. However, he could stay away no longer, as the leave he had asked for was not given willingly.

'I must go to London, Mr Eldon, but I would be obliged if you would keep my room free as I intend coming back in two days. I'll send you a telegram if I'm going to stay any longer.'

Richard's house was in Clapham, a fast-growing village about five miles out of the centre of London. It was a humble two-up, two down terraced abode on the south side of a common. He put his key in the lock and went straight into a narrow hall with a staircase opposite. He turned into the main room and dumped his bag on the floor. He walked back into hall and went to the scullery, fetched a jug and went to the pump that served several houses. He filled a kettle and put it on the range in the front room. He took a spill from the container on the high mantel and putting a match to it, poked it through the bars to kindle the fire he had laid before he left. The range was highly blackened. It had always been kept so by him and Christopher after their mother's death, as it was a new addition and her pride, as were the two china dogs and clock. There were two alcoves, one on either side of the chimneybreast. In one was a low wooden built-in cupboard with a crocheted runner on top and various ornaments of his mother's. In the other was a small bookcase that his brother had made as a sample piece when he was apprenticed. The wooden floor was bare apart from a small rag rug in front of the fender.

He sat down at the square, chenille covered table and watched the flames take hold. To his surprise, tears began to well in his eyes as memories of his brother and parents and his happy childhood in this house suddenly hit him. He had never left home to visit any other part of the country, just trips to London to see the sights with his parents when he and Christopher were children. Now he had no family, no close friends, no one to talk things over with or get advice. He could not return to live here, it would be too painful. He had to start a new life as his brother had suggested. Richard quickly brushed the back of his hand across damp cheeks and told himself he was a very fortunate person despite this feeling of isolation.

Nevertheless, fortunate though he was to own a house, it did present problems. His short stay in Kent had left him with this desire to settle there. Had his brother not urged him to travel? He could get a position in an accountant's office in Tunbridge, he was sure. He did not fancy the gypsy life, wandering rural England seeking work where he could. Anyway, would that not be a waste of the education that his brother had so diligently paid for? In addition, lurking at the back of his mind was a desire to do something for Grace. She had no family and neither had she his advantages. It did not seem right that she should have to live the way she did through no fault of her own. But then why should he be so upset about her? Hundreds of children were exploited and much worse off than Grace was; down mines, up chimneys, working in factories for hours and hours in dangerous conditions. That Lord Shaftesbury was trying to do something, he had read. Grace did have the benefit of better food now than she would have had before and the air was fresh - he grimaced - well fresh if you were not living too near the station.

He would have to give up his job and sell the house and these thoughts sent his mind into a whirl. He looked over to the range where the water was boiling and he went into the scullery and reached for the tea caddy. He peered in. There was just about enough to make a small pot of tea. He was not likely to have occasion to buy any more as at around ten pence a quarter, it was an extravagance. He remembered his mother telling them how expensive it was when she first bought some and he and Christopher had always used it sparingly.

Richard sipped his tea. Giving up his job would not be a problem, but selling the house - where would he start? You needed a lawyer or solicitor, did you not? He would have to look along The Pavement or the High Street in Clapham. Maybe John Eldon could advise him? He was in the building trade and probably knew about such things. Richard turned out his pockets, putting the coins to one side. He searched for the leather pouch hidden inside the top of his trousers, where he kept a five-pound note. He could live on that for a while until he got another job. He frowned. He would have to go to the bank though, that was where he had the money that Chris had left him. He was not sure how much, about £20 he thought. He was determined after Chris died that he would live on what he earned. Those savings were meant for travelling, but now he had considered selling a house and buying another, it would probably all go. He had no idea what such transactions would cost. He sighed, stood up and drained his tea, then went upstairs to pack a bag with fresh clothing ready to return to Kent in the morning.

'It's a good job you've returned,' greeted the publican as Richard passed him in the flagstoned passage between the tap room and the kitchen. John Eldon brushed the dust from his hands on his trousers. 'My wife has had a hell of a job with Grace since you went.' He bent close and whispered, 'Yesterday she started her courses - you know.'

Seeing how discomforted John was, Richard guessed. Not having any sisters, he was not absolutely clear exactly what was entailed, even less why he was being consulted.

'Er, how does it concern me?'

'You see,' John went on, still speaking quietly as if the whole inn were listening, 'she doesn't believe anything Jane tells her and Grace said you were the only one she *would* believe. If you say it's true, then she would know it was.'

'Isn't there some young woman - a friend - who can explain?' he asked, anxious not to be involved in such a delicate matter.

'She says she'll only speak to you.'

'I will talk to her, if you think that'll help, but I would like to see your wife first.'

Mrs Eldon and Richard went into the stables. 'You wait down here, Mrs Eldon. so you can hear what she says.'

'Grace,' he called. 'It's Richard. May I come up? Mrs Eldon tells me you're not feeling – that you want to speak to me.'

He heard her mutter something as he climbed up and sat so his head was just below the loft floor, not wishing to upset her by going too close.

'Don't you feel well?'

'I had a pain, but it's gone.' She sobbed. 'But dere's blood - it's everywhere. I'm going to die, aren't I? I've got de fever, like my mother.'

'No, of course not.'

'Mrs Eldon says it's natural, but I never heard 'bout it. She's just saying dat?'

'All young girls of your age have – er, have something – er - every month.'

'Every month!,' she shrieked. 'Every month! I won't have any blood left so I'll die anyway. I knew Missus was telling me lies.'

'In that case why are there any ladies left in the world?'

Grace contemplated this piece of information. 'So it's true what she said?'

'Yes. She wants to help you, to explain all about - about what happens. You're a young lady now.'

'Are you sure it's all right?' Grace insisted.

'Yes, I'm sure. Mrs Eldon's here and she will tell you what to do. When you feel happier, we'll go into Tunbridge and I'll buy you something. Would you like that?'

Grace sniffed and wiped her nose on her sleeve and he heard a scrape as she pushed her treasure box out of sight as he began to descend.

'Mrs Eldon.' Richard dropped his voice and lowered his eyes, too uncomfortable to look at her. 'Do you think you could get Grace to clean herself up. This would seem a good opportunity.'

'I've tried, heaven knows I've tried. But she's a very stubborn girl.'

'I've also spoken to her about washing, perhaps you could try again.'

'You'd think, being a country girl, she'd have known about - about this sort of thing,' Jane Eldon said with a sniff.

'Yes, I would, but I suppose her mother had not got around to explaining.'

Richard hastened back to the inn, quite flustered about the whole episode. He felt he would not be able to look Mrs Eldon in the eye ever again without blushing and poor Grace, even allowing for the fact she admired him, must have felt confused and distressed.

'Is Grace convinced?' John asked. He was washing his hands at the pump.

'Yes.' Richard hurried on. 'Mr Eldon, I would like your advice. You carry on your work as a builder, so I thought you might know what is involved in selling a house. When I was back home I took down the names of two solicitors in Clapham, but didn't enquire further because I didn't know what to do.' He shuffled his feet.

'Why? Have you got one to sell?' John asked, laughing at such an unlikely idea.

'Yes, I have.'

'Good gracious, young man. There aren't many lads of your age in such an advantageous position.'

'It's very unusual I know even to own a house, let alone at my age. It's all thanks to my grandfather, I gather, who lived very frugally, and left my father enough, well nearly enough money, to buy a property. But I'm a bit ignorant about such things because my brother, who was several years older than me, dealt with any money matters after my father's death. It's all paid for.'

'Why do you want to sell it?'

'I thought I would buy something here - in this area. I know I've only been here a few weeks but I've grown to like it.'

'I fancy a house would be cheaper here than in London.'

'That's another good reason for moving,' Richard said.

'There's a great deal of building going on in the south of the town near the station. Several farms have been sold recently, but there are a couple of empty places in Three Elm Lane. I'll find out who the owners are and take you to look them over if you like, see how habitable they are and what is being asked for them.'

'Is it very complicated selling a house?'

'No. I just think you have to deal with someone reputable.'

'Yes, I see.' Richard was not sure if he would be able to tell who was, and who was not, reputable - that was the point.

'I'll enquire, shall I?' John said, noticing his puzzled expression.

'I would be grateful. I'm not very worldly wise I'm afraid – a bit like Grace.'

John laughed. 'A bit better than Grace I hope.'

Next day Richard returned to the hopgarden and though he was faster than he had been on his first days, he found he had lost his rhythm and had to work up speed again. The weather was still fine but was getting colder as they were well into October. One evening, after his meal, he walked to Tudely. One thing he had learned to do was walk, and going into Tunbridge was no longer the ordeal he had once found it.

It was dark as he walked along the Hartlake Road which was narrow, muddy and winding, with several of the funny buildings he had noticed on his arrival. They were called oast houses he had learned, and Richard now knew they were relatively new buildings for drying the hops. He stepped on to the narrow bridge over the Medway and at the crown leaned over the somewhat rickety wooden fencing and peered into the strongly flowing river. Not far away he could discern a barge going towards Maidstone and, in the distance a small boat with its red sails just visible.

Though it had not rained for the last two days, the water was still high and beginning to lap the banks and spread into the meadows where large pools were forming.

He left the bridge and continued towards Tudely. The majority of hops had been gathered in; the poles looked stark and some dead leaves clung forlornly to the poles like perching birds. Richard could hear singing in the distance and as he approached the sound he saw people round a bonfire. He recognised them as the Irish travellers. They worked near him in the garden and were a bit like the gypsies in that they also travelled the country following the harvests of the changing seasons. He waved to them and was beckoned over.

'Sure, and how are you this evening, young man. We don't know your name?'

'It's Richard Wakefield. I'm staying at the Bell.'

'You sound like a Londoner.'

'Yes, I am, well just outside. How did you know?'

'Though we come from Ireland, most of us when we're not travelling around, live in or around London. I'm Dennis Collins and I live near Tower Hill.'

'I live in Clapham, south of the River Thames Do you know that area.'

'No I can't say I do.' He turned to the woman next to him. 'This is Mary Quinn.' Richard noted the pretty young woman around twenty, with auburn hair falling in thick waves down her back, 'and that's Catherine Clare with her son over there.' He indicated a young woman and a boy of about ten close by. Dennis lowered his voice. 'Catherine's been recently widowed, so she has. We persuaded her to come down with us – to have some company.'

Richard thought Catherine Clare an attractive woman in a sad sort of way. Her hair was auburn, too, but lighter than Mary Quinn's and her eyes, when she looked up at him, were pale blue like his own. He smiled as he held out his hand.

'This is my son Patrick,' she said. Richard moved his hand towards the boy who had his mother's red hair, but he bowed his head. 'Shake the man's hand, Patrick,' his mother said giving him a nudge.

'Pleased to meet you, young Patrick. I like that name. Do you like hop picking?'

He nodded shyly as he took Richard's hand.

A small woman introduced as Margaret Mahoney, asked if he would care to join them and have some food.

'Oh no, no thank you. I have eaten and I don't want to intrude. I was just out walking, something I used to do little of when I was home. What do you do when you've finished here?'

'Different things. Some might stay to pick apples and later dig potatoes. Others mend pots and pans, or make tin plates. They might work their way up to London.'

'I go to Covent Garden,' piped up an older man. 'I buy peas and cauliflowers and broccoli and sell them round the streets.'

'Is that so.' Richard said. 'Then I shall look out for you if I'm ever that way.' Then he remembered he was not intending to be in London in the future. They took up their singing as he left.

Further on were wooden barns and open sheds where the last London pickers had gathered in the open and were cooking over a fire. Some, Richard had heard, lived under disgusting conditions and some out in the open under hedgerows, like the ones he had seen when he first walked into Tunbridge with Grace. How did they manage in the pouring rain, he wondered? He would have liked to continue to the gypsy encampment, but he had been told they would not welcome him in their midst.

Had he continued he would have seen the gypsy families each gathered around their respective tents surrounded by their animals and carts. Two dogs were chained nearby. The tents were made of sailcloth thrown over bent hazel rods and there was a little opening at the top to let out the smoke if they had to cook inside.

By the Leatherland tents the women were occupied with the meal, preparing the vegetables and skinning a rabbit. A kettle pot was slung over a fire and the vegetables and herbs were thrown into the pot along with the pieces of rabbit.

'What do you think of that Richard Wakefield?' Samuel said to his son-in-law.

'He seems nice enough for a gorgio,' John said. 'Centine likes him. She's always on about the man.'

'He likes children, I can tell,' Samuel said. 'That chai he brings with him sometimes, he seems to like her. Don't care for the way she talks to him. No woman of mine would speak to a man like that.'

'Fanny's taken a liking to him,' John said mischievously.

Samuel nearly cut himself on the knife he was using on a woodcarving.

'Dordi, dordi! She'd never marry a gorgio – I wouldn't allow it. We'll find a husband for her. One of the Taylors, I think.'

John laughed. 'I don't think she has any intention of marrying a gorgio but I've seem them look at each other.'

'And that's the way it'll say. I shall keep an eye on her and you do the same,' he said sternly.

Charlotte moved behind Samuel. 'Here's the money I collected today.'

Samuel put down his knife and took the coins from her. He pulled out a leather drawstring purse and dropped the coins in.

John reached into his pocket. 'Here, this is what I got.' He dropped the money into his father-in-law's purse.

'Do you want any money for anything?' Samuel asked John.

'Not yet, but when I start on the wheeled vardo, I might ask then. When we get to London we must draw up some plans.'

'When I see how your vardo works out,' the older man said, 'I shall make one for us.'

CHAPTER 4

Richard was having breakfast when someone came into the room. He glanced up then returned to his meal.

'Hello, don't you know me?' Grace grinned at him.

Her long hair had been washed and glowed a beautiful gold and was tied back with the ribbon he had bought her. Her face and hands were spotless; her clothes neat and clean. Mrs Eldon was standing behind her, a smug demeanour replacing the usual grim one.

'What d'you think to this young lady, then?' she said.

He opened his mouth, shut it, and opened it again. 'I don't know what to say.'

Grace blushed and looked down at her feet where her transformation had not extended to shoes, though they and her feet were cleaner.

'How are you feeling now?' he asked.

'I understand it all now Missus has explained - and I can have babies?' she said, as if such a thing were imminent.

Richard laughed. 'When you are older I hope, Grace. Now, I suppose, I shall have to buy you that present?'

'Don't get too carried away, my girl. There's still work to do,' Mrs Eldon said sharply, but even she was delighted at what she considered was her handiwork.

'When can you spare her? I need to go into Tunbridge on business soon, and we can go together. She shows me where to go and what to do.'

'Tomorrow - it's Saturday, isn't it? She can get some shopping for me at the same time.'

Elias Jones, the carrier, was going into Tunbridge and for a penny ha'penny, he said he would take Richard and Grace. Richard was pleased, as he did not fancy having filthy shoes if he was going to see the solicitor that John Eldon had recommended.

After passing the toll, the cart turned left into Swan Lane and past The Hermitage, a large, elegant house Richard thought he would like to live in. He jumped off the cart outside The Swan and helped Grace down. They waved to the carrier as he left them.

'Let's go to de wharf and see if we can see barges loading,' Grace said, 'I like watching dem. There's so much more happening here, better than Golden Green. I 'spect Lunnun has lots going on all de time.'

'Yes, I suppose it does. However, people have to work. It's not all standing around.'

Grace obviously did not agree. 'When I've saved enough money I'm going to Lunnun.'

'Oh, yes, and what do you intend doing when you get there?'

She hesitated. 'I'll- I'll get a job.'

'From what I know, Grace, you won't be paid much, you'll have to work seven days a week with little time off. You're much better off in Kent than you think. Life can be very hard in a big city like London.'

She shrugged her shoulders convinced he was wrong.

They turned left into the High Street and stopped outside a factory beside the river. Richard looked in the square-paned window where various sized wooden boxes were displayed. Different woods that looked like mosaic depicted local scenes. He stared, fascinated. Shown by his brother at various times, Richards was quite knowledgeable about different woods and their colour and grain, but he had never seen this type of work before.

'Do you like these?' Richard pointed.

'Dey're all right,' she said, disdainfully. 'What'd you do with dem?'

'They're beautiful, don't you think? I wonder how they're made? My brother would have been fascinated. Did I tell you he was a cabinet maker?'

She was not impressed by the boxes or a cabinet maker brother. In her opinion if you could not wear it, it was not worth considering. Richard, on the other hand, liked ornaments like this.

For fifteen minutes they watched two barges on the opposite bank to the factory - one loading hops from the wagons lined up in the street past the Rose & Crown, the other off-loading coal. Three men of massive build were standing talking by the barges.

'Who are those men?' he asked Grace.

'What men?'

'Those three standing over there - built like houses.'

'Oh dem, dey pull the barges.'

'Pull the barges.' Richard exclaimed. 'They pull them all by themselves!'

'Yes, aint you seem 'em before?'

Richard shook his head in disbelief. He would make a point of going to the bridge in Hartlake to watch them. Fancy pulling a loaded barge all the way to or from Maidstone.

They crossed to the other side of the road and watched the animals drinking from the horse wash. They were overseen by boys who had been given a farthing to keep and eye on them while their owners went for a drink in the nearby Chequers. Tunbridge seemed to Richard to have an endless number of inns and beer houses, even more than in Clapham.

'Now, Grace, where do you think we can buy shoes?'

'There's a woman what sells old things in Ninepin Alley.'

'Where's that?'

'Up 'ere.' She pointed towards the town hall.

They passed The Chequers and walked into Back Lane, close by the castle.

'Dat's where my friends went,' she said, as they passed a grim, four-storied building. 'It was de workhouse, but de've moved it somewhere else now, Pembury I heard, but I don't know where dat is.'

'It's not so bad working for Mrs Eldon after all then? You could be with them.' Richard looked down at her and she gave a grin, not wanting to admit that was true.

An elderly woman stood behind a table in front of her hovel. Her clothes were no cleaner than Grace's had been a week ago, and her hands were ingrained with dirt. Sensing the likelihood of a sale, she began picking out shoes and boots, which she thought might be the right size for Grace.

'You wants dem large 'cause her feet will grow,' the old woman said to Richard, handing Grace a pair of boots.

'What do you think?' he asked.

'Where dey come from?' Grace shrewdly asked.

'A man gave them to me – both dese pairs.'

Grace did not believe her and turned her back and whispered in Richard's ear that they probably once belonged to some poor soul that had died in the workhouse, and the old woman had stolen them.

'Try them on, young lady.'

Grace leaned against Richard to remove her own grimy boot and put her foot into the one the woman passed to her. She screamed.

'What on earth's the matter?' Richard exclaimed.

She pulled off the boot and tipped it up. Out fell a dead rat. Grace flung the offending article from her.

'I'm not 'aving dem,' she said, hobbling away.

With one muddy shoe in his hand, Richard hurried after her. 'Well, where shall we get some? I can't afford to have new ones made for you, if that's what you're hoping for.'

'I didn't think dat,' she said indignantly. 'Would you like a dead rat in your boots?'

'All right, I'm sorry. Where else do you know?'

Eventually they found another house with a trestle table outside. This had a great deal of footwear, some of it nearly new, as well as laces and stockings. Eventually Grace decided that a pair of black boots were suitable and Richard bought her a pair of white stockings to go with them.

'There, now you'll look smart from top to bottom. Keep them clean.'

'Why you so worried 'bout keeping clean? Nearly everyone I knows is dirty. They gets dirty doing deir work like I does and dey don't have water to waste on washing, or other clothes to change into.'

'I'm sorry, I didn't think. I just don't like being mucky. I suppose I get it from my mother. She always made us wash and she kept our clothes clean and we had to brush our shoes. And the gypsies, they and their clothes are always clean, haven't you noticed? And they live outdoors most of the time.'

'All right, I'll try. But it's not ter'ble easy 'cos I aint got anything else.'

Richard sighed. He could see that one day he would be buying her another set.

'Look, Grace, I'm going to the solicitors now.'

'What's a solicitor?'

'I want to sell a house and you need a ...'

'Sell a house? You got an 'ouse? A whole 'ouse that's all yours?'

'Yes, but I don't want to live near London anymore. I'm going to live down here, and I need a solicitor to help me.'

'You don't want to live in Lunnun!' Clearly Richard was out of his mind.

'I like it here.'

Grace stared at him in disbelief, and was about to say something, but clamped her mouth shut.

'Now what are you going to do while you wait for me?'

'I'll sit on the horse trough and watch people get out of dem carriages at de Rose and Crown. And the mail coach'll be coming soon on its way to Hastings. I can see what dem ladies are wearing.'

'You'll soon look as smart as them, at the rate you're going.'

'I don't think so.' She laughed.

John Eldon had recommended John Cannell because, he said, he had a good reputation in Tunbridge. He told Richard that the solicitors had been in the town since last century, so he was sure he would be dealt with in a professional manner.

Richard walked up the High Street and saw Bridger's, the printers. John said it was opposite. He went through the gate and up a long, straight path to the double fronted building. He opened the door into a small porch and pulled off his cap. He hesitated, wondering if he should knock or go straight in. The decision was made for him when a messenger boy came out and held the door open.

The office appeared much like the one where he had been employed previously. One clerk of around fifty was sitting at a desk; he looked more important than the other two who were perched on high stools in front of a long sloping desk. Above the desk were brass rails on which rested large leather-bound ledgers and sundry papers tied with pink cotton tape. Around the room were bookcases and more shelves with bundles of parchment.

'Yes, young man. What can I do for you?' said the clerk peering over his spectacles.

'I – I want to speak to a solicitor, Sir.'

'Do you have an appointment?' he asked brusquely.

'Er, no, sorry. Must I have one?' Richard was embarrassed at his lack of knowledge of procedures. The clerks at the desk sniggered.

'Get on with your work.' Immediately pens were dipped into inkwells. 'What is it in connection with?'

'I want to sell a house.'

Senior Clerk, probably ascertaining there might be money in the offing, tempered his unsympathetic manner.

'What is your name? I'll see what I can do.' He stood up and moved importantly towards another door, returning a few moments later.

'Mr Cannell will see you now,' he said, his tone implying he was lucky to be seen at all.

Mr Cannell was an affable-looking man in his mid fifties. His florid face was bewhiskered to his chin. He greeted him in a familiar manner, which rather startled Richard. Was it the thought of the money he might bring, or was he that way by nature?

'Do sit down, Mr Wakefield.' He indicated a chair in front of his desk. 'Mr Norris indicated, somewhat sceptically I might say, that you want to sell a house? Can that really be so, you are so very young?'

Richard was getting a bit annoyed at being told how young and how lucky he was to have a house. Unusual it may be, but he could not be the only person of his age to have been so fortunate.

'Yes, Sir,' he said, more sharply than he intended. 'I do have a house, it's in London and I want to sell it and buy one down here. And no, I don't have any relatives, it's all mine and it's paid for.'

The solicitor coughed, and Richard realised how rude he must have appeared to such an important man

'I do apologise, Sir, but everyone keeps telling me how fortunate I am, as if I didn't know.' He went on. 'It was John Eldon who recommended you to me.'

Mr Cannell frowned. 'Eldon, John Eldon, you say?'

'Yes, he's a builder and innkeeper with his wife at the Bell at Golden Green.'

Oh, yes. Yes, of course.' Richard was not convinced he did know who he was talking about. 'Let me take down a few details.'

'Do you live far from the centre of London?' he asked Richard as he reached for paper and a pen, and moved the oil lamp closer to him.

'Five or six miles.'

'Anywhere near the Great Exhibition?'

'I did manage to go to it.'

'You did!' Mr Cannell exclaimed, placing both hands on his corpulent stomach, where his gold watch chain and fob lay. 'What was it like? I meant to go myself but never did. Was it as exciting as the newspapers said?'

Yes, Sir, it was amazing. Made me very proud to be a citizen of this country. The stands from the Empire were awe-inspiring.'

'It was quite expensive to get in, wasn't it?'

'I went on the shilling day, so it wasn't so bad.'

'Good, good. Now what you must do is find a buyer for your house - advertise in the local press or put an advertisement in a shop nearby. When you have done this find out if this buyer is using a solicitor and let me have all the details. If all goes as planned, the money will come to us and be put in an account on your behalf, then, when you have found a suitable place down here, come and see me again, and we'll set things in motion.'

It all sounded a bit too easy to Richard. 'But what shall I ask for my house?'

'See if you can find out what has been sold in your area recently for a similar abode. Look in newspapers, that will give you an idea.'

'Ye-s, thank you, I'll do that.'

'Nice to meet you young man. I'll see you again soon..' Mr Cannell stood up, went to the door, and opened it.

'Mr Norris, see this young gentleman out, if you please.'

'You've been a long time,' grumbled Grace, pulling her ragged shawl close about her. 'It's cold standing here.'

'You're a proper misery sometimes,' Richard said. 'I've just bought you a pair of shoes and stockings and you're still moaning. I suppose the next thing you'll want will be a coat?'

Grace stared at him, not sure if he were joking or not. Mr Cannell had indicated that selling and buying a house was not quite as expensive as he had anticipated and, with the likely price discrepancy between his London home and one here, he would have money to indulge himself – or Grace more likely.

'Come on, I'm in a good mood so, before it wears off, let's find something to eat and then we'll look for a coat of some sort.'

Grace grabbed his arm with both hands and skipped down the road beside him.

'You spoil that girl, Mr Wakefield,' Mrs Eldon said on their return, gazing after Grace as she went to the stable. "No good will come of it, you'll see. She'll cost you a smart penny before she's done and when she's had enough out of you – and us – she'll be gone. You mark my words.'

'Surely you don't begrudge her a few clothes,' Richard said, believing Mrs Eldon was jealous. "They are only the minimum she needs.'

'She wouldn't have that if it weren't for John and me taking her in,' she sniffed. 'She'd be in the workhouse, that's where she'd be, or begging in the streets.' And with that, Jane Eldon flounced into her kitchen.

Mrs Eldon disapproved of their relationship, having told her husband she thought "it wasn't quite right" and "what about that other business" without elaborating, but John assured her Richard was one of the most honourable young men he had come across and she was never to express her opinion in the tap room. People would soon make a mountain out of a molehill.

It was the last day of hop-picking for Mr Cox, and some of the gypsies had already broken camp.

'I shall miss you, Samuel,' Richard said, 'I shall miss you all, especially little Centine, even though I can't understand a word she says.' He looked over to where the family were standing.

Samuel smiled. 'We will be in the area for a few more days, but if we don't see you again, we'll meet next September, that is if you're still going to pick hops.'

'I shan't be picking hops, but I shall be here all right. I'm buying a property.'

Samuel looked surprised but made no comment.

'Are you walking back to your camp now?' Richard asked Fanny who was standing next to her father.

'Yes,' her father answered for her. Samuel glanced around him to see where his family were, and then signalled they should move off.

'Goodbye till next year,' Richard called to them all and waved. Fanny held back a little and he saw her look to see if her father was likely to turn round, but he was deep in conversation with his wife.

'Well, Fanny, I shall miss you.'

'I shall miss you, too,' she said, without looking up at him. 'You said you were not going to pick any more, but will you come and see us next year?'

'I'll try, but I shall be working during the day. Perhaps on a Saturday, if I finish early.'

Fanny stared after her family. 'I hope so.'

Her father turned round, and sternly beckoned her., 'Fanny!'

'I must go. Good bye - Richard, artch boktalo at behtalo.'

He did not know what it meant, but it sounded friendly.

Richard sold his house in Clapham with ease, much to his relief, and the money was in Beechings Bank in Tunbridge, Mr Cannel told him. John Eldon had taken him to see two prospective places in Three Elm Lane and today he was taking a second look at the one he had liked more. It was the last of a row of three cottages in Three Elm Lane near the Hadlow road to Maidstone. In front of the cottage there was enough room for a few plants against the wall under the window. Richard was wondering if it were worth putting anything there as any plant would soon be covered in mud from the passing waggons and carts.

John Eldon put the key in the lock of the stout wooden door and they entered the main room. The walls were of whitewashed stone, and there was a small, bleak-looking range on the right of the room. Richard thought of his mother's immaculate one at home and felt a tinge of sadness at leaving the only place he had ever known, and its associations with his parents and brother. He gave himself a shake; no use having regrets now.

'Come through here, Richard.'

He followed John into a scullery, which had a deep sink and a wooden floor cupboard beside it. There was a small walk-in pantry with shelves on three sides and on one of the shelves was another cupboard, which had wire mesh in the door.

'This seems adequate for my needs,' Richard said, gazing around trying to imagine it with a lived-in appearance.

John unlocked the back door and they went into the small garden. 'There is just about room for you to grow your own vegetables, maybe keep a chicken or two.'

'I wouldn't know how to look after them.'

'Grace'll show you.' He gave Richard a cheeky smile, then continued. 'There's a well at the end of the terrace that serves all three cottages, and the water is fresh.'

Richard was pleased to hear that. 'What about sewerage?'

'There's a cesspit at the bottom of the garden and the privy's over there.'

Richard opened the privy door to see a closed-in wooden seat with a hole in it and a bucket underneath. It did not smell too unpleasant – but then it was empty. Sewerage disposal was better in London, at least where he lived it was.

'What do you think of the construction?' he asked John as they went inside.

'I looked it over yesterday as best I could,' John said. 'The roof is leak-proof and the stonework appears to be well constructed and in good condition. The walls are sturdy; the ceiling is lathe and plaster, which will need attention periodically. With a cottage of a fair age, you must expect there to be some deterioration that you will have to deal with from time to time.'

'I shan't mind that,' Richard said.

'May I ask how much you want to pay?'

'Not more than eighty pounds.'

'You should get it for less than that. In the south of Tunbridge, new terraced houses are going for £90 and bigger villas for £120, I hear. Let's go upstairs.'

Back in the main room John pointed to the range. 'Do you see that, it was once an open fireplace but when the new modern range was put in, it was blocked up on one side.'

'Yes, I see. Something similar happened in our house but I can't remember the change. Before I was born.'

To the right of the range was a door. John unlatched it and they climbed the winding wooden staircase. There were two bedrooms and on the landing was a tall storage cupboard. Richard studied each room. The only drawback he could see was getting the place dried out. It smelled musty and damp because, John said, it had been empty for six months at least. 'The owner died, I believe and his son is selling it. I've got the name and address here in my pocket.'

As they went downstairs, Richard said, 'I think this will do very nicely, John. I'll go into Tunbridge tomorrow and set things moving with Mr Cannell.'

A few weeks later and much quicker than Richard had surmised, he was standing once again with John Eldon, but this time in his own cottage.

'Well, what do you think? Are you pleased with your purchase?'

Richard gazed around the room, before saying, 'It's smaller than my house in Clapham. Ceiling's a bit low.' He touched it with his hand. 'But it's cosy.

'You shouldn't be so tall.' John said and grinned. 'As I said, it's in good condition considering its age. Just let me know if you find anything that wants doing.'

'I am grateful to you for all your help. Everything went so smoothly, I was quite amazed. Mr Cannell was efficient and I have some money in the bank. Did I tell you that my brother wanted me to travel the country and then see the world? But I think I'll stay here for a while. I've taken a liking to Golden Green.'

'We shall be very pleased to have you living here permanently. But what are you going to do – for work, I mean? You are not so wealthy as to be a man of substance, are you?'

'Far from it. I shall be seeking some sort of office position next week.' Richard gazed about the room. 'I've my furniture coming soon, but I shall need other things like curtains. Do you think Grace will be any good helping me?'

'I wouldn't think so. You'd be better off enlisting Jane's help. I'm sure she would be willing.'

Richard was not sure he wanted Jane Eldon to help him. She seemed a bit too austere for his liking but, then again, she would cast a practised feminine eye on things. 'I'll see. I can't move in yet, as I have nothing to sit or sleep on till the carrier comes from London, then I must pay your bill. I have been most grateful for your hospitality and advice.'

'And it has been a pleasure to have you staying. Jane and I hope you will be happy here.'

The range fire was burning nicely, taking Richard's mind off the snowy scene outside. Beneath the front door a thick sausage wedge lay keeping the draught at bay. He looked around the room with satisfaction. All his possessions from Clapham had arrived undamaged. A new sideboard was opposite the range and the table, covered in his mother's chenille tablecloth, was in the middle of the room, the four chairs placed neatly underneath. The rag rug stood in front of the fender, but he thought he would buy a big carpet to cover the stone floor which, he hoped, would alleviate some of the coldness. He had asked Grace to blacken the range in the living room. The china dogs and clock were on the mantelpiece which reminded him of home. He kept the fire going night and day and left the door at the foot of the stairs open and he lit a fire in his bedroom for several days to dry it out. Mrs Eldon had proved to be a great help, had made curtains and had even come to put them up for him. Grace had washed and swept and cleaned as if it were her own home, and together they had walked into Tunbridge and she helped him stock up his pantry.

'You ought to dig your garden now,' Grace had said, placing some eggs in the pantry. 'Then you can sow seeds and also grow potatoes.'

'You are a slave driver, Grace. Do you know that?'

'And you're an old softie Lunnuner.'

'Not so soft now I can walk into town and back, and I'm no longer a Londoner.'

Yes, he was going to be happy here. Christopher would be very proud of him.

CHAPTER 5

It was next evening, when Richard came finally to settle his bill with John Eldon, that his wife greeted him. Perhaps, not so much greeting, more like haranguing.

'She's gone. I told you she would. Fat lot of good you buying her all those clothes. Now she has what she wants she's off. Just like I said.'

'Wait a minute, Mrs Eldon. Do you mean Grace? Where's she gone?'

'How do I know? I didn't see her this morning so I went over to the stable and called, but there was no answer. I climbed the ladder – not a sign.'

'But she wouldn't just disappear without telling anyone? Why she was as happy as anything when she helped me in the cottage and ….'

'Well she has. There's no bounds to her.'

'….and yesterday,' Richard went on, ignoring her interruption, 'she was with me at the cottage and she gave no sign that she was unhappy and wanted to run away. Perhaps she's gone into Tunbridge to spend some of the money she earned hopping?'

This obviously had not occurred to Jane Eldon, but she was not to be pacified. 'She could have told me. I don't know what the world's coming to. Young people have no respect nowadays.' And she flounced off into her kitchen convinced Grace would never be seen again, and muttering, 'After all I've done for her.'

Richard was not convinced on either move. She might have gone into town, but he thought it very unlikely, and as for running away - no definitely not.

He crossed the yard and went into the stable. At the top of the ladder he looked around. Since he had last been there a great deal of hay had been removed but she had still made herself a cosy alcove. Richard hoisted himself on to the floor and moved the blankets to one side. With the tips of his fingers he felt under the hay to see if her box were still there. It was. He opened it to find the length of ribbon he had bought her, two pearl buttons, five separate shillings and tuppence three farthings in coppers.

Richard shook his head. Surely she would not run away without taking her precious box and money, and if she were going into Tunbridge Grace would at least take the coppers. He pushed her box out of sight and sought out John Eldon, who had just finished work for the day.

'How are you getting on?' Richard asked.

'Nearly finished. Then I'll put in a front door on the road and people can come in that way as well as from the stabling yard.'

'It'll make the place much bigger. You should do more trade.'

'I hope so.'

'I've been to see if Grace left anything that would suggest she had run away, but she hasn't taken any money at all,' Richard informed him.

'How do you know?'

'Because I know roughly what she had from picking, which was five shillings. She hasn't even taken the few coppers that were there.'

'What about the coat you bought her?'

'I didn't notice it, though her shawl was still on the floor. It's February, so she'd need her coat.'

'It's very strange,' John said, as he went to the pump and worked the handle until the water came gushing out into a bowl. He rinsed his hands and splashed his face. Richard handed him the rough towel that was on a bin nearby.

'I'm going to look for her,' Richard stated.

'What tonight?' John exclaimed.

'The quicker the better don't you think? She can't have gone far if she's heading towards London on foot, and if someone has taken her....' Richard could not bear the thought that she had been kidnapped. She was an attractive girl; there was no knowing what might happen to her if she were in the hands of some unscrupulous person. 'I'll go back to the cottage now and then set off.'

'But you don't know which direction she might be headed.'

'I know, but London is the best bet.'

'Well if you're intent on this I suggest you take a short cut to the London road. Go into the Hadlow Road, past Tanyard Farm, and you'll come to a track on the right that goes up past Cage Farm. Keep heading across the fields until you come to the road. You'll know it's the London road because there'll be more traffic on it. You're going to get very muddy so put on a stout pair of shoes and take a change of clothing. You don't know how long you'll be searching. Anyway there will be hostelries on the road. You might even get a ride on the mail coach if it's not full.' He flung down the towel. 'I must say rather you than me. It'll be like looking for a needle in a haystack. I think you're mad.'

It was nearly eight o'clock when Richard left his cottage. He found an old pair of shoes which he changed into and fetched a shirt and his only other shoes and stuffed them in a bag to carry on his back. He had hurriedly added some bread, a piece of pie, cheese and an apple. He might be travelling through the night, if his premonition was correct that Grace was heading towards London. As he came out on to the Hadlow road, he wondered if he were mad as John Eldon said. He could be roaming the London/Hastings road for days. How was she travelling? On foot? Certainly on foot if she were alone; but if she were with someone else, what transport had he at his disposal? It was deathly dark, with few vehicles on the road to Hadlow. One consolation it was not raining and, for winter, it was not particularly cold or windy.

Taking the track past Cage Farm, Richard reached the London road an hour later and turned towards London. He passed Hilden House where a coach had stopped. No point getting on the coach even if there were room. He was sure that being on foot would prove more fruitful. How long had Grace been gone? She was seen last night around nine-thirty to ten o'clock, so that would be twenty-four hours at the most. He strode on and the coach rumbled past him. On the other hand, she could have gone in the early hours of this morning.

Richard felt very vulnerable walking in the dark. Everywhere in London where he needed to go at night, there were gas lamps. Here in Kent he had rarely been out after dark.

He tramped on. Every hostelry or beer house he passed he searched inside. He reached the Cock Horse, where the last of the drinkers was leaving good-naturedly.

'Have you seen a young girl wandering around this area?'

'What sort of age?'

'Fourteen.'

'Runaway?'

'Could be, but I don't think so.'

They looked at each other shaking their heads.

'Have you seen anything strange like a man and a girl together, a reluctant girl?'

'No, haven't even seen anyone strange in here tonight. Sorry.'

Richard felt despondent already and he had only just set off. What had he expected, that Grace would be waiting for him somewhere? He said, 'By the way, what's the name of the next town on this road?'

'Sevenoaks,' shouted a man over his shoulder as they dispersed.

Sevenoaks, he discovered, would come after another steep hill. He was feeling weary. Should he seek a sheltered place to sleep, or walk on into the town? The sleep appealed more and he found on a bend of the hill, a spot off the road in a dip. He piled leaves all around himself and settled for the rest of the night.

It was the sound of a coachman shouting at the horses that woke Richard. When he had eaten, he resumed his journey up the twisting hill. The town was waking and beginning to bustle. The road divided by a horse trough. He went into an ale house called The Chequers and noticed through the window there were a few stalls on the other road that had gone to the right. He stocked up on food to see him through the day and asked the stallholder which of the dividing roads was the one to London.

'The main London road is through that alley,' she said.

Richard did not think Grace would have got this far on her own. He did not know why he felt it, but he was convinced she was with someone.

He ploughed on through the day and to his dismay, yet another longer and steeper hill lay ahead. His feet and legs hurt, and his back had not taken kindly to the previous night's sleeping position. Perhaps he was the softie that Grace so often accused him of being, but it was at the top of this hill, at a beer house, he thought he might have a breakthrough.

'Pint please.'

The tankard was put in front of him. 'That'll be tuppence.'

'Have you seen a young girl, fourteen, fair hair? She may have been with someone.'

He shook his head, but a man near him said, 'There was a man in here last evening. Nasty looking chap, never seen him before.'

Richard perked up. 'Was there a girl with him?'

'Not that I saw, but he was certainly behaving strangely. Kept looking over his shoulder, shifty like.'

'Yeah, now you come to mention it, he was a bit peculiar,' agreed the landlord. 'Asked if we had anything to eat he could take with him.'

'And there was no girl with him – outside perhaps?' Richard asked hopefully.

'I didn't go outside to see,' said the landlord.

The other man said, 'There was no one there when I went home about fifteen minutes later.'

Encouraged, Richard questioned the landlord about the road ahead and the next town he might encounter.

'Bromley's the next big town; it's a fair way. The going from here is very bleak. I wouldn't advise you to travel it in the dark, if I were you. It's wooded, and it's darkening already.'

'Have you a room for the night?' he asked.

'We don't do bedrooms, but I have an empty room. It's a bit cluttered, but if you don't mind, you can have it for thrupence.'

'That'll do fine. I shall be leaving very early in the morning so I'll pay you now.'

Richard left at six. He made good progress and judging from the terrain, he was glad he had not gone any further the night before. It was deeply wooded on both sides of the road, only the traffic gave it a feeling of normality in the daylight.

There were people travelling on foot, some pushing barrows and small carts, making deliveries in the locality. There were larger carts delivering farther afield. One man sitting on his red and blue waggon had stopped to eat his breakfast. Richard enquired from him what he had seen on the road.

'I set off early from Sevenoaks, but I didn't see a young girl. Is she on her own? Not a good idea to be on her own, there are some....'

'Yes, I know, but I think she has been abducted by a man – could be a woman I suppose, but I don't think that likely.'

'What she look like, this young lady?'

'She's fourteen, average height for her age, fair hair. She was wearing a dark blue coat, black boots, white stockings, and a long dress with an apron. She might have had a white cap on.'

The waggoner shook his head. 'I've not seen anyone like that. I tell you what, young man, if you'd like to hop up beside me, I'll give you a lift. You'll be able to see better up here.'

Richard climbed up gratefully, thanking the carter profusely. What a bit of luck. Twice they stopped when Richard saw first a lone girl, then a man and a girl, but neither time was it Grace. Nearing Bromley, they passed a man pushing a barrow.

'I think I'll question him,' he said. 'He might have seen something.'

The waggoner called 'Whoa' and Richard jumped down.

The man caught them up and went to go round the cart.

'Excuse me, but have you seen a girl, about fourteen with fair....'

'No, I aint.'

'She could be wearing a blue coat, dark....'

'I told you I aint seen no girl.'

Richard climbed disconsolately back on to the cart.

'He was a bit abrupt,' the waggoner commented.

'I'm sorry to stop you like this.'

'Don't you mind about that. Glad of the company.'

In Bromley Richard bade farewell and went to find an eating-place. It was as he was coming out of the shop the same man with the barrow passed. He thought he saw a movement beneath the carpet that covered the contents. He was about to challenge the man once more, but thought better of it. He would follow him instead.

There were big houses on both sides of Bromley's main street and a few shops by the Market Square. Richard stopped at a stall and bought cold meat, bread and fruit, trusting the man would not get too far ahead, assuming he would be staying on the London road.

Unfortunately, as he left the town he did not catch up with him. Frantically, he wondered if he should wait a while in the hope that the man had also stopped. Or had he turned off? He stamped his foot with frustration. John had been right. What a fool he was. Grace could be on her way to Hastings or Rye or anywhere miles from here. The only thing he was certain of was that she had not run away.

He approached a woman inadequately dressed for the bitter weather, with a pinched-faced child holding her hand.

'The turning I passed,' he pointed back the way he had come, 'does that go to London?'

'Yes, through Beckenham village, but you can still get to London on this road.'

'Yes, yes. Thank you.'

Convincing himself that the man and his barrow had not come this way, Richard retraced his steps and walked down a steep, twisting hill. How nice it was to be going down for a change, though it was not doing much for the calves of his legs.

Greatly relieved, he saw the man in the distance, and a girl. A girl! Could it be Grace? She was about her height, but she was not wearing a blue coat. At the bottom of the hill was a small hamlet where the man had stopped. He saw him roughly haul the girl into a shop.

Richard caught up and leaned against the wall outside until the man came out. It was definitely Grace.

'Grace?' he called softly as they came out of the shop.

She turned dull eyes to him as she was dragged away.

Richard called to the man. 'Hey, you. What are you doing with that girl?'

The man turned. 'What's it got to do with you? She's me daughter.'

'What's her name?'

'Mind your own business.'

'It's Grace, isn't it? Where are you taking her? She lives with the Eldons now.'

'I know where she lived, but she don't live dere now. She's with me.' Grace looked at Richard with eyes that were blank, though her brow was furrowed as if trying to remember. The man pushed Grace towards the barrow and put her in.

Richard went after him. 'I'm going to the police.'

'And what dey going to do?' he sneered. 'I'm her father and I can do what I like, so you can go back where you come from. You're wasting your time. Get out of me way.'

The man strode off unconcerned and Richard sat on a milestone proclaiming ten miles to London, and put his head in his hands.

What *could* a constable do, that was the point? If the man was her father, she belonged to him, even if he could prove she was being ill-treated. Even then he doubted if anyone would listen to him. Were there police in the country? They had them in London - but here?

Richard's eyes were brimming. He wished Christopher were here, he would know what to do. His brother's advice had often been sought and taken. He, Richard, was just a silly, inexperienced young lad, setting off into an evil world about which he had little knowledge and, thankfully, no experience. His brother would think as John Eldon had, would he not, that Richard was stupid even to try to rescue Grace? In deep despair and physically weary, he succumbed and tears trickled between his fingers.

After a few moments he stood up. He was *not* going to give in. He had come this far so he might as well see what was going to happen to Grace and help her if he could. He bought milk from the shop and drank it straightaway. He bought two pies for the next day. He wanted a wash and a decent cooked meal, but he could not stop for long. He had to keep Grace and her father within sight, without being seen himself. If they stopped somewhere for the night he could perhaps stay at a lodging house. Trouble was, he would not know when they set off again. He would just have to deal with that when the time came. This, Richard supposed, was what the saying 'living on your wits' meant.

Grace felt strange - she did not know why. Sometimes she was lying down, sometimes walking. Why was she walking? Had Mrs Eldon sent her to buy something? And that man who spoke to her a while back, she thought she knew him but what was his name? Why did she feel so far away and who was the man walking with her? She thought she knew him too. He was very rough, kept saying they were going to Lunnun. She always wanted to go to Lunnun, she told Richard that. Who was Richard?

The man gave her something to eat and drink and she became very sleepy again and lay down in the barrow. The man covered her with something heavy. How nice to go to sleep, they would soon be in Lunnun, soon be in Lunnun, soon be....

Richard entered the mean and sordid streets around the docks in Rotherhithe. They were a maze of alleys. Mud and filth lay in the gutters where children, begrimed with dirt, played. The smell was oppressive. He had managed to keep a track on Grace the last few days and was convinced by her demeanour that she was being drugged.

Her father was ahead. He rested the barrow on its handles and took the carpet off Grace. He lifted her and tried to stand her up, but she could not do so by herself. 'Stand up, you stupid girl,' he shouted, slapping her face. He leaned her against the wall of a building but she slid to the ground. He swore, but left her and went into the dimly lit dwelling, one of many tall, dirty tenements along the alleys. Richard wanted to rush to her aid, but he had to keep his head and work out exactly what he could sensibly achieve.

Richard crept forward and looked through the dirty panes. Grace's father was talking to a large woman whose face was heavily rouged. Two girls of around Grace's age were sitting on chairs. They wore cheap, taffeta dresses that had been cut down to fit them and had seen better days. Their faces were also painted. Grace's father was pointing outside, and they moved towards the door. Richard scuttled across the alley and hid in a shallow doorway desperate not to be seen.

'You leave 'er 'ere, Mr Brandon. We'll soon teach 'er what's what,' she cackled.

'Yes, but what about the money? I told you I'd fetch 'er, and I thought we 'ad an agreement, like. It weren't easy bringing 'er all the way to London. Some man were looking out for 'er, but I shook 'im off.'

'Don't you worry. When she starts earning 'er keep, you'll get a cut. Or,' she said slyly, 'if yer can't wait and don't want nothing more to do with 'er, I'll give you a fiver right now, and you can forget awl about 'er.'

Grace's father frowned, weighing up the pros and cons. 'Look 'ere, I need to think 'bout this. I'll tell you tomorrer,' he said.

'I'll 'elp you get the young lady inside. Grace you say her name is. Nice. Might change it though - now she's starting a new life.' She sniggered.

They struggled with Grace's lifeless body and dragged her into the room. A few moments later Brandon came out, took up his barrow and left.

Brandon - so that was Grace's name. Richard had never known – never thought to ask. He viewed the disappearing Brandon from his doorway as he disappeared into the fast closing night. While he was trying to think what he could do next, two men came into the alley and made for the tenement where Grace was. One, a sailor, was drunk, the other sober.

'This is the place. You'll get good service here.' The sober one knocked on the door and they went in. Richard went back to the window to listen.

'Mrs Crabtree, good to see you again. This 'ere sailor wants a bit of entertainment. Needs to sober up a little, but he's good for a pound.' He winked. 'His ship's come in and he's just been paid, see.'

The woman shouted out, 'Leave that girl and come 'ere, Jen. There's a customer for yer.'

One of the girls Richard had seen through the window sidled up to the sailor who leered at her in a manner which made Richard want to vomit.

'Not fancy a girl yourself, Sam?'

'Not tonight. I've other work to do.' He put his head closer to Mrs Crabtree's. Richard strained to hear what he was saying.. 'Job at a warehouse. Could do with a bit of 'elp. Know anyone who'd be a lookout.'

'Can't say I do – oh, wait a minute. There's a man called Brandon who may be looking to earn a bit of money and not fussy where it come from.'

'Just what I need. Where can I find him?'

'He's only just left, pushing a barrer. You probably passed 'im, so if you 'urry you may catch 'im up. And when you're ready, I've a nice young piece just arrived that you might like to try out. Give it a couple of days. Beautiful girl.'

'Keep her by and I'll be back. Should have a bit more money by then. Look, here's a shilling. Buy her something pretty - that I'll appreciate too.' He gave the woman a dig in the ribs with his elbow, and they both hooted with laughter.

Richard was beside himself with rage at what this evil man could do to a young girl, to Grace. He could hardly bear it and wanted to rush into the hovel and take her from this squalid, depraved place; he wanted to smash the man's face and hurl him to the ground and kick him until he moved no more. So angry was he that he almost gave himself away as he made to cry out at these people who exploited the young and vulnerable for money. How could they? How could they treat human beings, children, for that's who they were, in such a disgusting and degrading manner?

Mrs Crabtree shut the door and Sam walked away, with Richard hurrying after him. He wanted to know what this 'warehouse job' might be. He dodged the grey washing that hung from building to building across the narrow alleys. He tried to avoid the indescribable items in the gutters and luckily avoided the contents of pots that were hurled from of the windows. Sailors crowded the nasty streets, most of them richer than they would be twelve hours hence. Ahead Sam went into a beerhouse called The White Hart and Richard followed. He saw Sam talking to a man with a drink before him. Sam beckoned a girl and ordered one for himself. The room was noisy and filled predominately with men, but there were a few women in garish clothes. Most of these were whores, getting their companions tipsy enough to rob them later. Richard touched the leather purse tucked inside the top of his trousers.

'Wot yer want?' A big bosomed girl asked Richard, making him start.

'Pardon?'

'Wot you want?' She eyed him suspiciously. 'To drink?'

'Oh, yes, to drink. Porter.'

'Pint?'

'Half.' Richard did not want a drink at all, but he would be conspicuous without one. He was better dressed than most of the customers, even though he was dirty and ill kempt after his journey. He wriggled uncomfortably in his seat.

Sam and his companion had their heads close together. They drew diagrams with their fingers on the table, and Sam took something from his pocket and showed it to the other man. Richard strained to see what it was. He was about to move to a closer table when Grace's father came in and hurriedly he had to turn his face away. Sam stood up and introduced Brandon to his friend. Richard longed to hear what they were saying but thought it prudent to move further away from their table. He would follow them when they left.

Through the gloom, Richard could just distinguish Brandon standing outside Colson & Co whose premises were on the dockside. This was almost certainly the building they were going to rob. He had lost sight of the other two, but Richard thought he saw one of them on the roof. Yes, there he was behind a chimney stack – and the other close by. Brandon looked around him and made a sign that all was still clear, and the men disappeared. Richard waited. What would they do now? How would they get in? Would they smash a skylight? A bit noisy; there were still people about, mostly sailors with their night companions. What were they going to steal? They would have a job getting goods out of a warehouse without causing suspicion. It must be money. Just then, the door of the warehouse opened. They exchanged a few words, then the men went back in, leaving Brandon outside. Would there be a Peeler in the vicinity? Now he *had* to get help - and quickly – and without being seen by Brandon. Richard slunk into the shadows. The church clock struck one. Where would he find a constable?

Grace began to rouse from her stupor. Where was she? Who was that ter'ble woman with the painted face – and that girl with bright red lips.

'Where am I?' she asked.

'It's yer new 'ome, me dear. Yer Dad bringed you 'ere.'

'But I don't want to be here. I want to go to my real home, it's in ....'

'It's 'ere now, dear. You'll soon get used to it, won't she Martha?'

'Yeah, you'll get used to it. Takes a bit o' time, but you'll get used to it.'

'Get used to what? Where am I?'

'You're in London, your father bringed you, like I said. Wants you to earn 'im a bit o' money.'

'My mother came from Lunnun,' Grace said, shaking her still muzzy head.

'Did she now? Then you'll soon feel at 'ome,' Mrs Crabtree assured her.

'Can I have a drink?'

'Get 'er some water, Martha.'

The girl left the room and returned with a handleless cup from which water seeped through a crack in the side.

Grace drank it gratefully, and wiped her hand across her mouth. 'Where's me Dad? I want him to take me back.'

'I don't think he'll do that, my dear. He'll be back tomorrer to get 'is money, no doubt. You just have a little rest and in the morning, Martha and Jenny will show you what's wanted. Jen's a bit occupied at the moment.' She grinned at Martha, who grinned back, with not quite the enthusiasm of Mrs Crabtree.

'Sir, sir, come with me. I think there's a robbery taking place. Down there.' Richard pointed. 'Come quickly, or they will escape.'

The constable eyed him suspiciously and straightened his top hat and uniform. 'You sure, young man? This is not some kind of trap? There were a couple of ships in yesterday, and you know what that means?'

Richard could guess, but he was not going to get into any explanation. He wanted something done about Brandon. He did not care about the other two, but if they were caught, so much the better.

'I'm not going down there alone, young Sir. I'm going to get a colleague. You wait here.'

'Please, please hurry or they'll be gone. It's Colson's warehouse. I overheard them plotting. Do you know it? I'm not sure I'll be able to find my way back as I'm a stranger round here.'

'So what are you doing in this part of London?'

'Please Sir, I beg you to get your colleague, or more than one. I saw them at the door. Hurry or they will be gone.'

Whether the constable was moved by Richard's entreaties or just wanted to get rid of him he was not sure, but he left Richard, telling him to stay exactly where he was. It seemed a very long time he was waiting, then two police officers arrived with the one he had spoken to.

'Right, Colson's you say. And you heard them plotting this robbery?'

'Yes,' Richard said, hurrying beside them. 'I heard them say a warehouse job, which didn't mean anything to me, then I saw them, three men, drawing diagrams, and, and…' Should he say he followed them? Would they not think it funny he was so interested. The police officer did not pursue the matter and they arrived close to the building. 'Course, they might have gone by now,' the first policeman said. Richard hoped this was not so, but it seemed to him, standing there on tenterhooks, that the peelers had taken their time.

'You keep out of the way in case they get nasty,' he said to Richard. 'We'll wait a few minutes and if they don't come out, Garrett, you can go round to the left, Davis you round the back, I'll keep watch at the front.' He turned to Richard. 'Do you know how they got in?'

'No, but two of them were on the roof, so they….'

'Skylight, no doubt,' he muttered.

'You said there was a lookout. Where's he?'

'I don't know. He was walking up and down outside when I came to find you. Look, there he is.' Richard pointed out Brandon who was adjusting his trousers as he emerged from an alley. They shrank back into the shadows.

'We've got to take out this one before he can warn the others,' he whispered. 'Garrett, think you can tackle him from behind?'

Garrett nodded. He crept forward keeping close to a wall and when Brandon turned with his back to him, he grabbed him, clamping a hand over his mouth. Brandon struggled and nearly got away. Richard could stand it no longer and rushed from his hiding place before he could be stopped. Garrett still had his hand over his mouth, but was having difficulty restraining a strong and stockily built Brandon.

Richard faced him full on. 'This is from Grace,' he said, punching him in the stomach so that he was forced from Garrett's arms as he doubled over. Richard brought up his fist again, 'and this is from me,' and he gave him an upper cut that had him fall back into the officer's arms unconscious. Richard went to hit him again but was restrained.

'I think he's out cold. Stand by him Garrett; me and Davis are going to find the other two. I think we've been quiet enough to catch them unawares. Young man?' He searched about him. 'Where's he gone? We might need him as a witness?'

'Don't know, Sir,' he said, laying the prostrate Brandon on the ground and putting his foot on him, 'but he didn't 'arf pack a punch. Slight man like him; didn't look capable, did he?'

As soon as the three police officers were preoccupied, Richard had slipped away. He had to find his way back to Grace and the maze of narrow streets confused him. Eventually after traversing alleys and lanes, he found the shuttered White Hart and traced his way from there. He knocked on Mrs Crabtree's door. The tenement was dark. A flickering candle light appeared in the downstairs room. He peered through the window, but could not see her.

The door opened. 'Who's there? Wot yer wanting this time o' night?'

'I want Grace?'

'Grace? Grace? There aint no Grace living 'ere, so clear orf.' She went to shut the door but Richard stuck his foot in and pushed past her. He peered around the grimy room. 'Her father left her here against her wishes and I've come to take her back home.'

'I don't know nothing abaht....'

Richard pushed the woman away and went to the foot of the staircase in the corner. He called. 'Grace, where are you? Grace?'

'Look 'ere, what you think you're doing? I'll call the police.'

'I don't think so, Mrs Crabtree. Grace's father has already been arrested for burglary and if you say anything to them, I shall tell them you were involved and knew all about it – not to mention all your other crimes, like kidnapping.'

'I aint kidnapped no one.'

'No?' Richard called again. 'Grace, come down here. It's Richard.'

He saw a shadow on the wall and Martha appeared at the top of the wooden staircase with a candlestick in her hand. 'Wot is it, Mrs Crabtree?'

'Fetch that young girl down 'ere. I don't want no trouble on 'er account. There's plenty more where she come from.'

Richard threw her a look of disgust and barely prevented himself from spitting in her face. If she were not a woman, he would have meted out the same as he had to Brandon.

A few moments later Grace appeared sleepily rubbing her eyes. 'Richard. Oh Richard, is it really you? These people say I must stay here, but I don't want to. Take me back, take me back with you.' She threw herself into his arms and cried.

'You don't have to stay here any longer, Grace. I'll take you home.'

'What about my father?'

'Don't worry about him. I think he and his friends might be taking a long trip on a convict ship. I'll tell you about it when we get you back home.'

Richard turned to Mrs Crabtree. 'If I were you, I'd keep very quiet that you knew Sam and Brandon. And if I ever hear that you've taken any girls against their will, I shall tell the police that you arranged the whole thing.'

It was unlikely he would ever know what Mrs Crabtree was doing in the future, but he liked to think he had frightened her.

'But I never did no such a thing,' she said, highly affronted.

'Good. Then you have never seen this girl, have you?'

'No, I aint never seen this girl.'

Richard said to Martha. 'Do you want to come with us, and the other girl?'

'Will you look after us?'

'No, I can't do that? But you could make a fresh start away from this life.'

'Nah, we don't know no other life. We aint never been to school, wouldn't be able to do nothing else.'

'As you please, but you could do better for yourself if you tried.'

Martha smiled. This man obviously knew little about life in the streets of London in the eighteen fifties.

Richard was a hero. The bar was crammed with regulars, as well as others who rarely patronised the Bell, but had heard of Richard's exploits. Everyone wished to hear about his adventure in London. Grace was the centre of attention, much to her delight, Richard thought. Two women were talking to her on one side of the taproom and the men to Richard on the other.

'She certainly owes a lot to you, Richard,' Robert Mills observed. 'John told me what a fool you were even to attempt to find her, especially as you didn't know exactly where she'd gone. He even thought we'd never see you again either!'

'I was sure she hadn't run away and I couldn't bear to think what would happen to her if she were abducted. My fears were justified, as it turned out and I thought London the best bet.' Richard shuddered when he thought of the revolting Mrs Crabtree and the evil fate that had awaited Grace.

'What's going to happen to her father?' 'Weren't you frightened?' 'What are the police like?' 'Do you think this shire will have a police force some time?' 'Will you have to be a witness at the trial?' 'How did you find your way home?' The questions went on and on as, fascinated, the villagers prised more and more details about his great adventure in the city none of them had ever visited, nor were likely to.

'I'll tell you this,' Richard said, 'we didn't walk back. We caught the train! I bet none of you have walked nearly all the way to London.'

They agreed and patted him on the back as they passed.

Richard glanced across the room and noticed that Grace looked very weary and was probably still suffering from the after-effects of whatever drug she had been given. He spoke to Mrs Eldon and she took her upstairs, and put her to bed on the sofa in her sitting room. When she had assured Richard that Grace was sleeping peacefully, he went home.

It was Richard's birthday and there were going to be celebrations in the bar that evening. It was Grace's birthday too, as no birth certificate had been discovered and there was no baptismal record at St Mary's. She told Richard she could not imagine her father even thinking about having her baptised. Richard told her he had been baptised at a beautiful church on the common in Clapham, and that if she wanted, she could be baptised as an adult. Grace took this in and shrugged her shoulders in familiar fashion when not sure what to say.

Since the inn had been enlarged, Grace had a room of her own. It was very small and had previously been used for storage, but it was better than the loft though not as warm. She had an iron bed frame with a lumpy mattress, her rough wool blankets, a counterpane and a striped pillow. There was a chair beside the bed and a marble-topped table on which stood a white bowl and matching jug. This table had two drawers where she kept her box, a comb, and her undergarments. There was nowhere she could hang her clothes, but as she had hardly any, they were tidily folded on the chair, and her shawl and coat were on a hook on the back of the door. Richard had bought her a bar of soap, which she used sparingly as she did not want it to go, but knowing Richard's thoughts on keeping clean she made sure she washed her hands and face every day. Now she earned some money, there was nothing to stop her buying her own soap, but she was saving hard to buy a silk dress, or even to have it made.

Grace crossed to the cracked mirror on the wall and began combing her hair. She wanted to look nice on this special day and she hoped Mrs Eldon would let her serve in the bar. Sometime she did, sometimes not, depending on whether there was anyone staying which involved her having to prepare, help cook and serve meals. There were bound to be many villagers tonight taking advantage of Richard's well known generosity. She was also excited because he said he had a present for her, but he would not tell her what it was. Grace had a surprise for him, too. It had cost a lot of money and that was another reason why she was saving hard. She was able to buy it because she was now paid two shillings a week and though she had once thought herself hard done by, Richard had made her realise how lucky she was to have decent meals and a job that was better than anything she was likely to get elsewhere, and her experience in London had brought that home to her. After putting on a clean apron and cap, she went downstairs.

'You'd like to be in the bar tonight, wouldn't you?' John Eldon said as she came into the kitchen.

'Yes, please. I want to see all that's going on and celebrate Richard's birthday. Mrs Eldon won't mind, will she?' she asked warily, wondering if it were Mr Eldon's idea and his wife had not yet been consulted.

'No, she's quite agreeable, and we can spoil you on your birthday, can't we?'

'What do you want me to do now?'

'Jane will be here in a moment, she'll tell you.' He paused, and then said, 'You are happy here? You aren't thinking of leaving, are you? We would miss you very much.'

Grace frowned. 'What makes you think I'm going to leave? I like it here.'

'Now Richard has taught you to read I thought you might want to get a position that's - that's, well where you could earn more money.'

'He's only taught me to read simple sentences, Mr Eldon. I can't read the newspaper because I don't understand what the big words mean, even if I can work them out. What better job could I get with that amount of learning? I am getting better though. Richard says I am a quick learner. So when I am Richard's age, then I can find a marvellous job.'

'That's all right then - till you're twenty-two at least.'

The air was thick with smoke and the main bar was crowded. In the tap room the older men sat by the fireplace, as they had when Richard had first arrived in Golden Green, most still in their smocks and working clothes. The two shepherds from Hartlake, Thomas Vanns the blacksmith and Joseph Smith, the wheelwright, were closest to the fire in their usual places. Set in their ways, they were reluctant to leave their cosy positions to go into the new large bar that John Eldon had recently finished. The younger men of the village had no such inhibitions and were pleased to have room to escape their elders, with their moaning about how different things were in their young days.

Grace was kept busy providing everyone with ale or beer that Richard had paid for. She hardly had a minute to appreciate the birthday wishes they bestowed on her. Perhaps when they had finished the free drinks, life would ease up a bit. It was nine o'clock before she had a moment free.

'Can you spare a minute? You have been so busy I thought you'd never stop.'

'I've got a present for you,' she said, her face flushed. 'I was going to bring it to your cottage this morning but I didn't have time. I hope you like it.' She handed him a small square parcel wrapped, rather crudely, with brown paper and tied with string.

Richard carefully undid the knots and removed the paper to reveal a small, square box with a lid. 'Why, Grace, this is one of the boxes we saw in Wise's factory window. How lovely.' He turned it in his hands, passed his fingers over the smooth surfaces and admiring the mosaic of various woods in a geometric pattern. 'It's so beautiful, thank you very, very much. I hope it did not cost...' He stopped.

She whispered in his ear, 'the man in the factory shop said it was a stamp box. I have saved up for a year.'

He gave her a kiss on the cheek. 'I think this box is wonderful and I shall treasure it always.'

Grace hovered, hoping that her present was forthcoming.

'I suppose you want to know what I have for you.'

Robert Mills came over. 'What are you two plotting?'

'Grace has just given me this box. It's from that factory by the river in the town. I told her I liked this sort of thing last year, and she remembered.' He glanced at the box again. 'I can't get over it.'

'But what have you got for her?' he asked, a sly look on his face.

Richard felt uncomfortable. He wanted to give his present to Grace without a lot of fuss. He did not want everyone to gawp.

'Mrs Eldon has it in her parlour. I shall give it to her when they shut.'

Robert was disappointed, but continued in his usual tactless way. 'I hear you've taught Grace to read. When do you do that - of an evening at your cottage?'

Richard frowned, annoyed at his innuendo. 'Are you implying that teaching her to read is a way of saying we are doing something we should not be doing?'

Robert looked flustered at hearing blatantly put into words what he had only meant teasingly to imply.

'Well, we haven't, and I would not think of doing such a thing. I come here to teach her when Jane Eldon says it's convenient, usually straight after I finish work. Grace comes to my house to clean when I am at work,' he emphasised. 'and, occasionally, she is very helpful to me with the garden and shopping. The least I can do for her is to teach her to read. She is quick and if she wants to I will give her some lessons in arithmetic. There, now you have our life history together, and I'll thank you not to give the impression to anyone that there is something improper going on between us. I won't have it, do you understand?'

Grace stood listening to this and then moved away. Robert stared in surprise. It was true he was making suggestions, but he meant it in fun. He did not think for one minute that Richard was taking advantage of Grace. He was not that sort of person.

'I'm sorry. I didn't mean to…'

'That's all right then.' Richard took up his tankard and quaffed the rest of his ale.

Grace skipped into the empty bar. 'Can I see it now everyone's gone? What have you got me?'

'Come on, let's go and find out where it's been hidden,' Richard said.

In the Eldon's parlour there was a large parcel on the sofa.

'There you are,' Mrs Eldon said. 'Richard's present. I'm sure you are going to like it.'

Grace went over to the sofa, sat down and put the parcel on her lap. It was soft to the touch. She tried to open it carefully, but was too excited and much to Mrs Eldon's and Richard's amusement she tore the paper from around it.

Her eyes grew large as she gazed at the folded pale green dress in front of her. She touched it delicately, looked up at Richard, then back at the dress.

'Hold it up then, girl,' Mrs Eldon's said. 'Let's see it properly.'

Grace put the paper on the sofa, stood up and lifted the dress so the skirt unfolded and dropped to the floor.

'Put it up against you,' Richard instructed.

'She can put it on,' Mrs Eldon said, as excited as Grace. 'Go into our bedroom.' She almost pushed her into the adjoining room.

Grace emerged a few moments later. 'Doesn't she look lovely?' Mrs Eldon said uncharacteristically.

'Do you like it?' he asked.

'Oh, Richard, you couldn't have bought me anything more beautiful. Do I look nice?'

Before he could answer Mrs Eldon said, 'Of course you do, doesn't she?'

'You do look lovely, as Mrs Eldon says.'

The dress was quite plain. Jane Eldon said it was not a good idea, in her opinion, to have a fifteen year old in frills and flounces. It would make her look like a prostitute. This he understood only too well, recalling Mrs Crabtree's establishment.

This dress had a round neckline, plain front and fitted into the waist with a broad band. It buttoned down the back. The long sleeves finished with a similar band at the wrist. In the candlelight the soft folds glinted, giving the skirt a striped effect.

'I don't know when you're going to wear it, young lady,' Mrs Eldon said. 'It's much too good to wear every day.'

Richard said, 'I shall have to take her to a concert in Tunbridge or Tunbridge Wells.'

'I'm going to Tunbridge Wells, I'm going to Tunbridge Wells,' she sang as she pirouetted and nearly bumped into John Eldon as he came into the room.

Feigning surprise, he said, 'Who is this young lady, Jane? Is she a guest staying here?'

'It's me, Mr Eldon. This is my present from Richard. Isn't it lovely?' She smoothed her hands down the bodice and spread out the skirt with each hand.

He stood back to admire it. 'You are quite the young lady now. You'll have all the young men wanting your company.'

Richard swallowed; Jane gave him a knowing glance; Grace blushed.

'Jane and I have bought you this,' he said, holding out his hand with a small parcel in the palm.

Grace unwrapped it carefully to find a brooch, with dark green glass stones in a circle. She stared up at the three of them. Then they all laughed as she said, tears running down her cheeks, 'I am so happy.'

CHAPTER 6

Richard said he thought he would like to learn to ride a horse. Grace laughed at this suggestion, and said he was really a softie Londoner after all and could not stand all the walking. He playfully cuffed her ear and said he should have left her in London if she thought that. He asked John's opinion on who in the village could teach him and what it would cost to learn.

John stroked his chin. 'The carrier can ride a horse, but I don't think he has wit enough to teach anyone. There's Miss White who's a good horsewoman. She lives near Style Place. You might have seen her, she sometimes rides past here; she might know someone.'

Not one to let matters rest, Richard set off to see Miss White the following day. She lived in a house that Richard thought very imposing. It was double fronted, built at the end of the last century, with a small portico and pilasters each side of the green front door. A maid, in a black dress with a white apron and cap, answered his knock. At his request to speak with Miss White he was asked his name, and shown into a room to the left of the hall. His hands began to sweat and he wondered if he had been too presumptuous to even call here.

Richard took off his cap. This house was more impressive than any house he had ever entered. The carpet, covering most of the floor, was red with a small blue pattern; by one wall stood an upright piano with two candlesticks extending from the frame. The lid was up and a piece of music was on the stand. He was tempted to go over and see what it was but a rustling behind him made him swing round guiltily. He found himself staring at one of the most striking women he had ever seen - comely was what his mother would have said. Her complexion was flawless, her features strong - straight nose, large mouth, firm chin. He could not decide if she were beautiful or not, certainly not of the same beauty as the gypsy, Fanny Leatherland. The contrast could not have been greater, not least in her dress, which was dark blue with pink vertical and horizontal stripes forming large squares. On her light brown hair she wore a small cap with delicate lace edging. He estimated her age as mid twenties.

Miss White eyed him from head to toe before saying, 'Mr Wakefield. What can I do for you? I am quite intrigued.' Her voice was low and well modulated. She indicated that he take one of the huge leather chairs that were placed on either side of the fireplace. She sat in the other.

'I, er, I want to learn to ride a horse and I wondered if....'

'I think you may have been misinformed. I am not a groom.'

'No, no. Not that,' he said, his face burning. His fingers ran round the inside of his cap. 'It's that I have been told that you are a good horsewoman, and you might know of someone who could teach me.'

'Ah, I see. And who was it that told you about my prowess on horseback? I did not know I was so famous.' A smile formed on her lips.

'John Eldon.'

'John Eldon from the Bell?'

'Yes. He said I could rent one of his horses, if it were not needed for other duties.'

Miss White did not speak for some time, convincing him he had definitely been too bold to come here. He stared around the room at the small tables of varying shapes and sizes, each with fringed coverings. Should he make his apologies and leave? Just as he was about to do so, she said, 'I had an instructor when I was about five, and progressed from there, but I do not know of anyone who could teach you.' She muttered something that sounded like 'Jakes maybe', then shook her head.

Another silence. Richard still did not know what to say or do next. He stared at the ormolu clock on the mantelpiece - four fifteen - it gave a strike to prove it which startled him.

Miss White rose from her chair and moved to the window, where an oblong table stood close by covered in plants dominated by a large aspidistra. Richard only knew the name of that plant because his mother had always said she wanted one. Miss White suddenly turned and came to stand in front of him. He jumped up anxious to leave the embarrassing situation.

'I have never taught anyone to ride,' she said. 'Let's discuss this carefully, shall we?'

An hour later after delicious cakes and the luxury of tea from a silver teapot and china cups, he left Miss White's house. She had agreed that she would give him lessons on Sunday mornings, after she and her mother had returned from church, and some evenings when he had come home from work while the evenings were still light. She also explained the need for a good saddle (was John Eldon's good enough, he wondered) and everything else to go with horse riding. It was all much, much, more than he had anticipated, and he should have deferred there and then, but he had fallen under the spell of Miss White.

'Keep your head up. Don't slouch. Knees in. Rise and fall with the horse.' Richard had tried to get to sleep while these words bounced around his head. His body ached and his muscles, not to mention the bruises where he had frequently fallen, cried out for relief. It was agony for him to turn in bed. He began to wish he were plump and not so tall, though he doubted that would have made his pain more bearable.

Grace, who had just arrived to tidy his cottage, said it served him right for having such grand ideas. 'Only 'igh class people go riding.'

'High, Grace, high, not 'igh.'

She looked down on him as he writhed in his new, wooden armchair. 'If I want to say 'igh, I'll say 'igh.' She thought he was getting above himself. She did not like the sound of this Miss White, had seen her out riding often enough and madam had not said so much as said a 'Good Morning' or nodded her head. But then her type never did. Grace stuck her nose up in the air. Bet Miss White would be surprised that she could read.

She did not want Richard to learn to ride. She was not sure why but supposed it took him farther away from her. But then again, it could not do much harm. Richard might take her into Tunbridge on a horse one day. She would like that.

Clarissa White was frustrated. Frustrated and bored with the restrictions under which she, as a woman, had to live. As her dear father had said many times, she should have been a man. Not that she wanted to be a man; there were *some* advantages to being a woman. No. What she wanted were the many privileges that went with being male. Her only interest, since her father had died, had been taking care of the family finances because she thought her mother quite incapable of dealing with anything more complicated than paying the servants' wages.

Septimus White had built up a brewery business and had left them nicely provided for, but even the modest fortune which he had accrued had to be managed and, being a shrewd and intelligent woman, Clarissa White was well able to cope. She knew that the solicitor and accountant that her father had employed were irritated, even intimidated, when she questioned them in minute detail when they put forward suggestions on where to invest her money. In fact, she was well versed in financial matters in general and hers in particular.

When her father knew he was dying, he had sold the business for a goodly sum because, he told his daughter, there will be no one to run it. She had pleaded with him that she could do it, but he would not be prevailed upon to entrust a mere woman to manage a firm, much as he admired her. This had left her even more embittered.

But now, the appearance of Richard Wakefield was proving to be a diversion she was enjoying. Her mother had ventured that it was beneath her to teach a common person, but Clarissa had pooh-poohed the idea, saying it made for a bright period in her dull life and who would know. Mrs White said no more, knowing it was pointless saying anything to her strong-willed daughter.

Richard had been learning for two months when Miss White asked if he would care to dine with them the next Sunday evening. He had only seen her mother fleetingly as he had glanced up at the house from the paddock, and saw her at a window. She was probably amused to see what a spectacle he was making of himself.

A new suit was called for, he persuaded himself. He only had the one he wore to work, apart from the old one he had cast off and used to wear indoors, and when that had reached a state that made it impossible to go out in public, a point it was quickly reaching, a new one was purchased. His present suit was only two years old, but was not good enough for dining with Miss White. So the garment was made up and hidden away in his chest, so Grace could not comment.

On the appointed Sunday Richard returned at six. He was shown once again into the drawing room. Miss White was waiting for him dressed in a peach silk dress with a layered skirt.

'Please sit down, Mr Wakefield. Would you like sherry?'

Richard had never tasted sherry but said boldly, 'Yes, please.'

Clarissa moved to a small table and poured two drinks from a decanter. She brought one over to him and sat opposite.

'You live in Golden Green, I believe, Mr Wakefield?'

'Yes, Miss White, I have a cottage in Three Elm Lane.'

'Rented?'

'No, I own it. My brother left me well provided for and I recently sold my house near London and bought this one.' Would this, he wondered, bring him up in her estimation?

'Really'. She nodded approvingly. 'You are very young to be in such an advantageous position.'

'So I'm constantly told. If I may say so, you, too, are in such a position.' This remark slipped out, and he wondered if such a forthright remark would bring forth a rebuke. He had learned whilst being instructed that Miss White had a very sharp tongue.

Before she could comment, however, the maid announced that dinner was ready, and it was only then that Mrs White came into the room. She was a small woman with a flat, rather sad-looking face. Richard could see no resemblance whatsoever to her daughter. They were introduced and then moved into the dining room, which was the other side of the folded doors.

The conversation was almost exclusively between Richard and Miss White who initiated every subject. Richard tried to draw Mrs White into the subject of horses, but apart from a comment that her daughter had always been a good horsewoman and how lovely the weather was in July, she added little else. Miss White ignored her mother as if she were not there, and Mrs White appeared to accept this. It made him feel uncomfortable. Richard had always been taught that one must respect one's elders, whatever station they held in life. Perhaps her mother was not quite right in the head, though he had not detected anything that confirmed this.

When the meal had finished, Miss White said goodnight to her mother who prepared to leave the room as if she were a naughty child being sent to bed. Richard stood up and bade her goodnight and she smiled sweetly and shook his hand, saying it was nice to have met him. Richard was not sure what to do when she had left. Should he make some comment? But he thought it better to wait for Miss White. He was her guest and not used to moving in such circles. He went to sit down again but she rose from her chair and Richard, who had been sitting opposite, sped round the table to pull out her chair. She gave him a smile which made his heart lurch and said, 'let's retire to the parlour. Would you like to smoke? I still have some cigars that were my father's if....'

'Thank you, but no, I do not smoke.' Richard's mother had forbidden his father to embark upon such a dirty and disgusting habit and Christopher and he had felt no compunction to take it up, even if they had been allowed.

He wondered what they would talk about in the parlour. Was this a different room or another name for the drawing room? It turned out to be the one on the opposite side of the hall.

'Your horsemanship is progressing well. Are you intending to buy a horse?'

'I'm afraid I could not afford a horse and its upkeep. No, I am happy to hire one from Mr Eldon whenever I want one. I would just like to ride occasionally; it appeals to me.'

'Yes,' she said, 'it is invigorating and one feels so free and unrestricted. I find it - yes, I enjoy riding. When you are more proficient and feel confident, we could ride out together on Sunday mornings.'

A moment of silence descended and he sought for something to say. 'This was where your father - where he conducted his business, I presume,' he said, gazing around the austere masculine room.

'I wouldn't say he conducted his business from here, but he used to discuss the brewery with me, even from when I was quite small. I couldn't understand what he was talking about until I was older, of course.' She looked wistfully above Richard's head. 'I was so upset when he wouldn't let me take it over.'

'It meant a great deal to you then, Miss White?'

'Indeed it did. One day I resolve to do something about it.'

Richard's cottage was only a mile and a half away, but in his quest to appear well-dressed, he had succumbed to having a new pair of shoes as well as the suit, and his feet were not taking kindly to the footwear.

He passed the Bell with the candles flickering in the bar and in the room upstairs. There must be a guest staying. He passed the last few houses of the village and it was practically dark and deathly quiet. He did not often venture out after dusk since he had been in his own home. If he wanted a drink and some company, he made sure he left the Bell while there was still some light. When the dark descended in the winter, he would not go out.

As he walked, he puzzled over what Miss White meant about 'doing something'. Doing what? In what capacity? Richard could not think of anything she could do in the way of a commercial project. Most women were excluded from such ventures.

What was his standing with Miss White? What did she think of him? She seemed eager to cultivate his friendship, but he could not see that *she* gained anything from it; he was certainly not of her class. It was obvious there had been, and still was, plenty of money to live in that house and manage its upkeep. Her clothes had been of the finest material, beautifully made; in fact everything about her epitomised wealth such as he would never attain. Yes, he said to himself as he put his key in the lock, she was a bit of a puzzle.

At the same time as Richard was musing over Miss White, she was sitting at her dressing table and removing her diamond earrings and necklace. She stood up and Susan undid the buttons of her dress and she slipped out of it.

'When you have hung that up you can brush my hair,' she said.

As Susan released the pins and took up the brush, Clarissa thought about the evening and Richard Wakefield. She had watched him carefully as they dined. He was well read, she could tell from the subjects she brought up and his comments. Moreover, if he knew nothing about a topic he was quite happy to say so. She had not probed too deeply into his background, but for one so young he appeared to have enough money behind him if he intended to ride regularly. He only lived in a small cottage in Three Elm Lane but she was surprised and impressed to hear that he owned it. His office wage would not be enough to sustain the life style to which he appeared to be aspiring. He was an enigma and one that she found intriguing.

'Ouch, don't pull so hard, Susan.'

'Sorry, Miss.'

'Do you know anything about Mr Wakefield, Susan?'

'Not really, Miss. He lodged at der Bell for several months when he first came to Golden Green, I think.'

'How long ago was that?'

'I'm not rightly sure, about a year I think, Miss. Do you want me to find out more? I know a girl what works for Mr Eldon.'

Clarissa closed her teeth over her bottom lip. 'Yes, you could do that, Susan. But be discreet.'

'ere, Grace, what do you know about Richard Wakefield?' Susan asked when she called at the Eldons for some eggs.

'What do you want to know for?'

'My mistress is interested. Seems to have taken to him. They had dinner together last Sunday,' she divulged.

Grace frowned and was about to say that Richard had not told her that, but she did not want Susan to know about her feelings.

'What she want to know?'

'She didn't say 'xactly, said to be discreet, whatever dat means.'

'I think it means don't go blabbing to everyone. In other words, just ask me what you want to know.' That, thought Grace, would keep her informed what Richard was up to with this woman. 'So, what do you want to know?'

'I don't know what she wants to know, I told you. I just said I would find out what I could, keep meself in her good books.'

'He comes from Clapham, that's near London, but he's moved down here now and bought a cottage in Three Elm Lane. He works for an accountant in Tunbridge. He bought me....' Grace thought it best not to give away too much. She also needed to be discreet.

Richard put a match to the fire he had laid. As the flames caught the paper and coal, and licked round the apple logs, he sat back in his armchair. Life was taking on complications he could do without. Everything had seemed so simple and straightforward after he had bought his home. He had managed to find a position with one of the three accountants he had found in Tunbridge. His position in Towner's was pleasant enough and the salary of one guinea a week satisfactory. In fact, more than he had been paid in London, but then he was older now and had more responsibility than he had previously. What had been troubling, apart from Miss White, was the amount of money he was spending from his savings. On top of renting the horse on the mornings or afternoons he wanted, and this cost roughly four pence for three hours, there were the extra clothes he had purchased including an outfit and boots which Miss White insisted he had to have if he intended to go out riding with her. He did understand her reasoning. Her riding habit was of fine brown wool, made up of a jacket with wide lapels caught in at the waist and spreading out over the skirt. The skirt was very full. Under the jacket was a cream brocade waistcoat with self-covered buttons from waist to neck. Topping this was a tri-corn hat with an ostrich feather trailing at the back. She would not like to be seen with a person wearing any old clothes and neither, for that matter, would he. While she had been teaching him, Richard had used his old office suit. Falling off repeatedly was not conducive to wearing the suit he had to work in.

At his first lesson he had been astonished when she had worn wide-legged trousers. He was even more shocked when she sat astride Mountaineer in order to demonstrate. When she saw his expression, she told him that she would prefer to ride astride all the time, but her mother said it was not dignified or ladylike to go out in public like that. 'For once I deferred to my mother.' she said. Richard was of the opinion that she liked the admiration she received when in public. She was a very attractive woman and Richard enjoyed being with her and seeing the envious stares.

What he did not like was being told how he should think. There were many things he could learn from the way she lived and she had opened his eyes by discussing with him political events such as the unsettled situation in France until Napoleon's coup d'etat the previous year. He knew she enjoyed putting him in his place and pointing out his ignorance on certain topics. He tolerated this, not only because he had little choice, but because he considered he was learning facts that he could follow up with his own study. If he was getting above himself as Grace said, so be it.

'There's an entertainment in Tunbridge Wells next Saturday afternoon. I was wondering if you would like to accompany me?' They had just returned from their Sunday morning ride and Richard was helping Miss White to stable her horse.

'Do you wish me to groom him,' he asked her.

'No, Jakes is back, he'll do it.' She gave Mountaineer a lump of sugar. 'Well, what do you think?'

'Yes, um, that would be a good idea. Do you know what it is - this entertainment?' Though the thought of accompanying her to Tunbridge Wells was enticing, he was conscious of the fact that he had not yet taken Grace out as he had promised on her birthday months ago.

'You do not sound enthusiastic?'

'Yes, yes, I am. Next Saturday you say. That would be delightful, but you do realise that I have to work until one o'clock, don't you?' Richard could see it had not occurred to her.

As he returned with Atlas, who had strayed to the far end of the paddock, she said, 'Would you care to stay for luncheon?'

'I don't think so, Miss White. I am not dressed well enough and I need to wash and....'

'We'll wait. Be back by one thirty; that will give you enough time to change.'

Richard mounted his horse. Now he would have to ask John if he could have the horse till later in the afternoon, as he would be unable to walk to his cottage, wash, change and walk back to Clarissa's in the stipulated time. More expense.

Back at the inn Grace met him as he hitched his horse to a hook.

'Enjoy your ride?'

'Yes, it was very pleasant. Would you like to learn to ride a horse?'

'I could never do that. Where would I find the money, or the time come to that?'

'But look how far you have progressed since I first came here. One day, Grace, I'm sure we will both have bettered ourselves.'

'Is that why *you* keep company with Miss White?'

Richard's face flushed. 'Er, no, I just like riding.' He looked around him. 'Have you seen John, I want to have Atlas for a little longer.'

'Oh, another ride this afternoon?'

'Do you know where he is?'

'He's in the garden.'

He hurried away, head down, unable to meet her eye.

As he was not as nervous as on the previous occasion, Richard had more time to take in the dining room at luncheon. It was slightly smaller than the drawing room, perhaps sixteen feet by fifteen. The wallpaper was striped crimson and royal blue, the curtains were of gold brocade with a fringed matching pelmet. In glass cases were stuffed birds on either side of the fireplace and on a round table was a paraffin lamp in a glass globe. Laid out on the mahogany sideboard was a collation of cold meats - slices of lamb, pork and brawn - and hard boiled eggs and tomatoes. In the centre of the table was a bowl of fruit containing oranges, apples and grapes. Richard was anxious to try an orange because he had only ever tasted one once before, and longed to have another.

Mrs White came into the room dressed in grey taffeta. On her head was a round grey cap with white lace edging that extended to tie under her chin. She smiled at Richard and held out her hand.

'Mr Wakefield, how pleasant to have you with us again.'

Richard took her hand and wondered whether to kiss it, but thought it might not be appropriate. He did not want Miss White to laugh at him. 'My pleasure, Mrs White. Are you well?'

Before she could answer Miss White said, 'Please take a plate and help yourself from the sideboard. Mother, do you wish me to serve you?' Her mother nodded and took her place at the head of the table as previously.

Richard savoured the smell of the food in front of him. There was enough there to feed a large family handsomely for days. He filled his plate, he hoped not too greedily, and stood behind his chair.

Miss White said, 'The concert is on at the Assembly Rooms. It begins with an overture *"Medea"*, an Italian soprano singing an aria and a Beethoven symphony, amongst other things.' She put her mother's plate in front of her and returned to fill her own. 'Do sit down, Richard. I can't remember everything. It should be good.'

'What is this, dear? Are you going to a concert tonight?'

'No, it's next Saturday. Richard is to accompany me.' Her daughter returned to her seat and began eating.

'That'll be nice.' She turned to Richard. 'Have you been to Tunbridge Wells?'

'Only once, Mrs White, but never to a concert. I was going to take a friend of mine....'

Clarissa's fork stayed on the way to her mouth. 'A friend. You have never spoken of a friend. Who is it?'

'Her name's Grace.'

'Oh.' She resumed eating.

On seeing the tell-tale sign of displeasure on Miss White's face, Richard turned to her more chatty mother. 'Did you ever ride a horse, Mrs White?'

'No, I have never ridden - well not properly. But I did have a pony and trap when I was little but it had to be sold because my father lost ....'

'Richard does not wish to know about your misfortunes, mother.' Duly chastened Mrs White contributed nothing more during the meal, and yet again Richard felt very uneasy and wondered why Mrs White did not assert herself more. Richard would never have considered speaking to either of his parents in such an abrupt and rude manner.

Miss White addressed Richard. 'Mother goes out visiting some afternoons if the weather is clement. Jakes takes her in the trap. I will get him to take us to the Wells, but I think a carriage will be better in case it rains.'

A carriage! That will be another great experience, Richard thought happily.

When lunch was over Richard took his leave saying he had to groom the horse before walking home from the Bell

'Now you can ride, have you reconsidered having a horse of your own?'

Richard almost laughed out loud. 'Miss White, you must have realised by now that I live very modestly, even though, as I told you, I am better off than most young men. I have spent my savings furnishing the cottage, on buying new clothes and the accoutrements that go with riding. I couldn't possibly afford to buy and keep a horse.'

'No, of course not. I was not thinking.'

No, he thought, your money does not have to be earned, it just arrives. 'What time shall I call here on Saturday?'

'I think it better that I call on you as we have to pass your home.'

CHAPTER 7

Susan was in the baker's in Hadlow when Grace came in. The late September day was unusually cloudless and warm, seducing people into lingering longer over their purchases. In fact, there was a queue and much gossip being bandied about, such as the goings-on at Hadlow Castle, Style Place, Fish Hall or any of the better establishments in the district. Servants were very good sources of information on such occasions. It never seemed to occur to the gentry that servants had ears and eyes.

'Dey going out to a concert in Tunbridge Wells on Saturday,' Susan informed Grace as they moved up the queue.

'Who? And don't say dey, say they,' Grace said automatically.

'Your Richard and the mistress 'course.'

'Saturday? To a concert?'

'Yes, dat's - that's what I said.'

Grace's face clouded. Richard said he would take her out so she could wear her new dress; she had no other time to wear it. How could he be so - so...? She could not think of a word. Had she not reminded him and he said he had not forgotten. Obviously, Miss White was more important than a promise he made to her.

'Dey - they seem to be very friendly nowadays.' Susan paid for her bread. 'He stayed to luncheon last week.'

'Did he.' Grace tried to sound unconcerned, unquestioning, as she watched her put the change in the crocheted pocket which was tied round her waist.

'I can't wait for you 'cause cook said to be quick,' Susan said, apologetically. Bye.'

When Grace had finished her shopping, she went up Church Lane to go home by the footpaths. On a whim, she went into the churchyard. Her mother was buried there. She looked around. Where? There would be no gravestone for her mother. She only vaguely remembered the funeral - how long ago - two years, three? She hardly ever thought of her mother - that quiet, submissive woman beaten by her husband on a daily basis when he was around. She kept out of his way if she could, but her mother seemed to accept it. She supposed she had pushed her mother to the back of her mind, as she had the hard, cruel life they both had with her brutish, drunken father. Did she perhaps despise the fact that her mother never tried to stand up for herself? Grace turned away sadly and followed the footpath through the churchyard to return home. However, she took a slight detour so she could pass the home of Miss White. It would take her a little out of her way but she could go home along the road instead of along the paths. It would be better for her boots. She looked down at them now, a bit dusty but they still looked smart. She rubbed each one on the back of her stockings.

Grace reached the Whites' house. Red brick, double fronted, central door with flat ridges each side. There were three windows upstairs and a roof in the middle that went up to a point and had a round window in it. No doubt Richard would tell her these had proper names. He had liked to tell her what things were and how to speak like a lady.

Suddenly she realised, for she was now old enough to realise, that there was no point in speaking like a lady if you were not one? She would never be a lady, she was common folk with a dead mother and a convict father. How could you live that down even if you were given the chance? Richard had wasted his time on her, and he now realised this. That was why Miss White was taking up the time he used to spend with her, when they studied his bible and he pointed to the words, told her what they were, and she had to say them. Richard told her how quick she was, even though she forgot sometimes, but most of the time she did not find it hard to remember.

She saw Susan wave a feather duster at her from a top window and raised her hand briefly, then strode angrily down the road to Golden Green through the hop gardens, many deserted as the pickers finished the drifts and moved to other fields.

'Richard!' she shouted out loud. He had given her lessons, bought her clothes, and changed her life. But he had passed on to higher things and she was not good enough for him now. She stamped her foot and the rolls nearly jumped from her wicker basket. 'Damn you.'

'Hello,' Richard said, as Grace let herself into the cottage. 'I've been hoping to see you.' He wanted to explain about going to Tunbridge Wells. He knew how eager she was to wear her new dress and show it off in public. It was not much for her to ask. He would have to study the local newspaper and see what entertainment they could attend.

'Have you?' Grace hurried past him.

He could see she was not happy.

'Yes, I wanted to tell you - to tell you - I - I need more candles.'

'But I only bought some a fortnight ago. I'll go and look.' She went into the scullery. 'Here they are,' she called, 'in the cupboard by the sink where I always put them.

'Oh, yes, I must have missed them.'

Grace studied his face, knowing what he was wanting to tell her, but too embarrassed to get the words out.

'I'm going to Tunbridge Wells ....'

'Oh, Richard, you are going to take me to the concert like you promised. How lovely,' she exclaimed, feigning delight.

'Er, well no. That is not what I wanted to say. I'm - I'm going with Clarissa.'

Grace noted the change of name. 'But you said on our birthday that you'd take me. Aren't I good enough now?'

'I will take you, it's just that she asked me - last week - I felt I couldn't refuse.'

Grace rolled up the large carpet in front of the fireplace and hauled it into the garden, refusing Richard's help. He followed her, but she pushed past him again as she came back for a hand brush and pan from a cupboard. She cleared away the ashes from the grate and reached for the coal and logs to re-set it.

'I am sorry, Grace. I didn't mean to upset you.' Guiltily he hovered, watching her, trying to judge her mood.

She emptied the ashes, returned the pan and brush to the cupboard, brought back a broom, and began to sweep the floor.

'Speak to me, please.'

'I have nothing to say, but if I did, I'm sure it would not be as good as something Miss White would say to you. Let me get on with my work.'

'But Grace, I really do care about you.'

'Do you? That's nice to know.' She replaced the broom in the scullery and went into the garden to vent her anger on the carpet thrown over the line.

He felt every blow.

Richard was eagerly anticipating the concert. Though he had not told Clarissa so, he had never been to such an event, neither had he been in a carriage. The journey was much rougher than he thought it would be. The roads were muddy and the heavy clay clogged the wheels as they climbed Quarry Hill. At the top Jakes had to get off and clear the mud from the spokes before continuing through Southborough village and into the Wells.

Nearing the Pantiles, they lined up behind other carriages to alight at the door of the hall. Jakes jumped off, opened the door, and pulled down the steps. Richard climbed out and helped Clarissa. She turned to Jakes saying as she did so, 'the concert finishes at 5.30, so try to be outside as quickly as possible, as I don't want to stand about waiting for you because it might be cold.' She put tuppence in his hand.

He touched his forelock, 'No, ma'am, thank you, ma'am. I'll try to be near de front early.'

Richard wondered if he ought to give Jakes something, but Clarissa had swept ahead. He gave Jakes an unreciprocated smile and followed her.

In the foyer, Richard took Clarissa's cape and left it in the cloakroom. The ladies in their off-the-shoulder gowns looked so elegant and beautiful. Richard had never been in such distinguished company. Clarissa's dress was of royal blue taffeta, which showed off her neck and shoulders. It tightly fitted over her bosom and into her waist. She had a beautiful figure and, being tall, her appearance was striking. Richard was very proud to stand beside her. The men were similarly elegant. Some men were in bright red regimental uniforms and these caught the eyes of the young women. The majority of the men were in frock coats, some with rich brocade waistcoats. Yet others were in suits with straight tailored jackets, as was his, but the cut and quality of the material was far superior, and Richard realised just how out of place he looked. This was confirmed almost immediately by a large lady bearing down on them.

'Clarissa, my dear, how nice to see you. Are you with your mother?'

'No, Mrs Deller, Richard here has accompanied me.' Mrs Deller scrutinised him from top to toe as Clarissa had done on their first meeting, then cursorily nodded her head. 'Richard and I go riding together,' she added.

Being in possession of a horse obviously retrieved his position as someone worth speaking to, in spite of his attire. Richard bowed and held out his hand. (He had just seen someone do this so thought he was on safe ground). Mrs Deller was won over as Richard touched his lips to her hand.

'So pleased to meet you. Doesn't Clarissa look beautiful?' she said.

'Yes, Mrs Deller, she is beautiful.'

They heard a bell ring and everyone moved towards the auditorium.

'Perhaps we shall see you in the interval, Clarissa. Basil is - ah, here he is. Basil, you remember Clarissa White, don't you? And this is her riding companion, Mr....?

'Wakefield,' Richard said.

They shook hands and Basil beamed at Clarissa, bowed low and lingered longer over her hand than Richard thought necessary. Mrs Deller noticed and grasped his arm. 'Come along, Basil. Perhaps we'll see you later Clarissa,' she called over her shoulder.

Richard was wriggling in his seat, like a small child eagerly awaiting a promised surprise. He studied the programme - an overture *'Medea'* by *Cherubini,* followed by an aria, *'Ah, mon fils'* by *Meyerbeer*. Richard was enchanted with the whole programme. His musical knowledge was non-existent, but he vowed he would go to as many concerts in future as he could afford. It went on much longer than he thought and included a concerto for violin, a *Beethoven* symphony in four sections, and another piece for violin, the concert concluding with a March. There was no interval and the concert finished three hours later. Jakes was dutifully near the Assembly Hall entrance and they were soon on their way home. Richard could hardly wait to discuss the music with Clarissa.

'That was wonderful. I have never been to anything like this before. I know little about music but I would like to know more. It was exhilarating. I couldn't get over the soprano's voice, it was so - so lovely.'

She glanced at him. 'I am glad you enjoyed it. We must go again some time.'

'Did I - did I disgrace you? I was not dressed as well as ....'

'Your charm made up for any deficiencies in dress. I could see several young ladies fawning over you.'

'No. You must have been mistaken,' he said seriously.

'I think not. I shall have to keep an eye on you.'

Jakes brought the carriage to a stop outside his cottage and he alighted.

'Goodbye, Clarissa, and thank you for a most wonderful afternoon.'

'It has been my pleasure. Till tomorrow morning. Au revoir.'

Jakes tapped the horse's flank and the carriage disappeared into the dusk.

Richard leaped in the air with delight as he thought of the music he had heard and the company he had been amongst that afternoon. He was rising in the world. How pleased his dear brother would be for him. He always wanted Richard to get on, financed him unstintingly and encouraged him at every important time of his young life. How he wished Christopher were here now to see his progress.

Next morning after church, when Clarissa had changed into her riding habit, she went into the parlour. She liked to sit in there sometimes; it reminded her of her father. She had loved him passionately.

Her thoughts turned to Richard. She *did* need to keep an eye on him. It would not suit her to have him distracted by some other woman. He was very personable and charming, and she was not ashamed to have him at her side. True, his clothes were not quite the part on occasions. Perhaps she could offer to buy him a better suit when they were going out in company together. She frowned. No, he would not accept that.

Her mother came into the room. 'Did Richard enjoy the concert? I forgot to ask you.'

'He did, very much, he was so enthusiastic. He said he had ever been to one before.'

'He seems very mature for his age. Didn't you say he was only twenty-two?'

'Yes.'

Mrs White said, 'I'm going to visit Mrs Spencer now. I will see you at luncheon, my dear. Is Richard staying?'

Her daughter nodded. Mrs White's comment about Richard's maturity brought to the forefront a scheme that had been on her mind for sometime; and Richard Wakefield would be the ideal person to help bring it to fruition. While waiting for him to arrive she went into the drawing room to the piano. She sorted through the sheets of music, selecting a march and began to play. Though she was an accomplished pianist, she pounded the keys in an unmusical fashion venting her feelings. She liked exciting things, things that tested her. That was why riding was important. If only her father had let her run the brewery - she could have done it with ease. He used to discuss the business problems with her, even asked her opinion, and occasionally had taken it. Why could he not see how capable she would have been? The sheet of music fell from the stand and she shut the lid with a bang, leaving the music on the floor.

Who was the friend Richard mentioned occasionally? Was it Susan's friend he had promised to take somewhere? She would have to ask Susan to make a few more enquiries. This girl might be a problem in her scheme of things. If she were a lowly servant girl, Richard should mind with whom he associated.

Clarissa and Richard were out on their normal Sunday morning ride. Some of the hop fields were still awash with pickers, much to Clarissa's disgust. He thought she must have got used to them by now, and hadn't they added to the small fortune her father had made.

He had progressed well in the last six months and she said it was time that he gave the horse a gallop. Richard was a bit anxious about this as cantering was about as fast as he had gone on their excursions As they came on to the Hartlake road, they chanced upon Fanny Leatherland near Thompson's Oast. Richard jumped down from his horse.

'Why Fanny, how good to see you again.' He grasped her hand and shook it.

She was taken aback by his effusive greeting, but said, 'We've noticed that you're not picking this year?'

'No, I work in an office now.'

'My father said you were going to buy a house last year, but none of us believed him.' She continued. 'I've been sent to Hadlow to buy some things for my mother, that is if they let me in the shop.'

Richard was about to remonstrate about this attitude to gypsies when the snorting of a horse made Richard turn to Clarissa. 'Clarissa, this is Fanny Leatherland.' He turned back to Fanny. 'Miss White is teaching me to ride. and I'm going for my first gallop today.' Fanny gave a slight bob.

Clarissa barely acknowledged that she had been addressed, and said, 'Shall we continue,' and turned her horse away.

Embarrassed, Richard hurriedly bade farewell to Fanny and quietly said he hoped to see the rest of her family before the picking ceased and they broke camp. He mounted his horse and raising his crop to Fanny, he cantered after Clarissa.

'I used to pick hops with her family last year, when I first came down here,' he said when he caught her up. 'They were so kind. I had entirely the wrong impression about gypsies …'

'Don't ever do that to me again.'

'Do what?'

'Speak to a common person - and a gypsy - while you are with me.'

Astonished, but with rising anger, he said, 'Fanny is not a common person. She is my friend and I do not ignore my friends at your, or anyone else's request. Now, do you wish to go home? If so, I will accompany you and then continue on my own.'

'No. We will go to the bridge then ride along the river bank to the East Lock and make our way home through Barnes Street.' She dug her spurs into her horse and set off at a dangerous pace along the narrow, winding road to the bridge. Richard followed at a more sedate speed.

Back in the paddock, Clarissa's face was like thunder as Richard dismounted and went over to help her. 'Do you wish me to stable Mountaineer?' he asked, knowing that Jakes was away ill.

'As you wish,' she said, and strode to the house.

Richard led her horse over to the stable near the house, took off its harness and saw him settled before fetching Atlas, who had strayed to the farthest part of the paddock, and riding him back to John Eldon's stable.

While he was grooming the horse, Grace came into the stable. He had seen very little of her since their tiff over the promised visit to Tunbridge Wells. Mostly, she cleaned the cottage on Saturdays when he was at work and they communicated by written messages. He was guiltily aware that he had done nothing about taking her out. They greeted each other warily.

Richard nodded his head, muttered her name and vigorously went on brushing the horse.

'Have I been looking after your cottage satisfactorily?'

'You know you have.' Richard gave Atlas a pat and went to attend to the tack.

'Thomas, you know, Thomas Vanns, the blacksmith's son,' Grace said chattily, 'he wants me to walk out with him. What do you think?'

'It's not up to me, is it? Do you like him?' He was taken aback and not a little jealous. He had not thought of Grace as having an admirer, which was stupid of him. He looked at her now with new eyes. Yes, Grace was growing into a very pretty young girl.

'He's all right. I don't think he'd knock me about like me dad did my mum.'

'I should think not. I'd have something to say if he did.'

'Would you?' She was pleased about that, but she also wanted him to be - to be a little more concerned about the situation.

'Of course. No one has a right to beat anyone else.'

'But you belong to your husband once you gets married. He can do what he likes.'

'You don't have to marry him.' Richard was getting tired of this conversation, and was still angry at Clarissa's attitude that morning. 'You can still be his lady friend.'

'But do you think it's all right, if we walk out?' She so wanted him to object.

'It's up to you. But don't get yourself into trouble.'

'Like you have today with Miss White?'

Richard was about to ask how she knew, and said pompously 'You know, Grace Brandon, you're far too disrespectful.'

'Should I respect you? You break promises.' Richard looked down at his riding boots unable to keep her gaze. 'Why are you here anyway? Don't you have luncheon with them on Sundays?'

'Miss White and I had a slight disagreement. I expect she'll get over it.'

'I wouldn't be too sure from what I've heard. She doesn't like to be crossed.'

'Who told you that?'

'Susan, her maid.'

'Oh.' He gave the horse another carrot and patted him on the neck. Was everything he did known in the village? Was there nothing sacred?

'I'll look in the newspaper and see what's on in Tunbridge or the Wells.'

'Better not tell Miss White,' she shouted as she headed towards the kitchen. But she wished that Richard had been a little more interested in her and Thomas, a bit jealous even. He just seemed - not interested.

CHAPTER 8

The same men gathered in the Bell of an evening to spend what little money they could afford, and what some could not. Drinking went someway to relieving the relentless monotony and poverty of their lives.

It was not going unnoticed that Thomas Vann's eyes followed Grace everywhere she went.

'Got a shine for her, aint you young man?' Thomas Willett, the shepherd from Hartlake, dug him in the ribs.

Thomas' face burned. 'No, I aint.'

'You can't fool us, young'un. Go on, ask her out.'

'We do go out,' he said feebly. 'We walks to the lane when she's finished.'

'Can't do much in that time. Why you've hardly enough time to give her a kiss.' The men laughed at his discomfort.

Grace came over with the ale they had ordered.

'This 'ere young man is a-dying of love for you, Grace. Put him out of his misery.'

'Why? What's he been saying?' She grinned.

'Nothing Grace, don't take no notice of dem.'

'Oh, so you mean I'm not good enough to go out with you?' she said in a serious tone.

'I don't mean dat. I - I -, can we meet when you've finished? Den I can explain.'

'Might be late, Thomas, especially if these men keep teasing you, and ordering more ale to keep at it.'

The men guffawed some more, but Grace took pity on him and whispered in his ear that she would walk with him, but she did not know what time she would finish.

It was ten when they finally got to walk back to his home that evening. When they reached the double doors of the closed forge Thomas turned Grace to him and gave her a tentative kiss. 'The men keep on at me, Grace. I don't know what to do to stop dem. If you become my girl - seriously, I mean - dey'll get fed up. Won't dey?' he added hopefully.

'You don't want to worry about them. If it wasn't you it would be somebody else. They like to tease you and the more you get upset, the more they'll do it.'

'But I don't like it.' He stared gloomily into the black, dank night, the only dim light coming from the front window of his house. 'Can we - can we go walking out together?'

'There's nothing to stop us.'

'I want us to be serious.'

'What do you mean by serious?'

Thomas was thinking about Richard who was always in the background.

'Just me, no one else.'

'Who else is there?' she asked, puzzled.

'Well, Richard Wakefield.'

If only he were a contender for her affections. Grace thought he was the most wonderful person she had ever met. Always so kind, knew everything, wanted her to better herself even though she was just a domestic servant. She could not imagine him losing his temper, not like the Missus who was always moaning about something and occasionally cuffing her about the ears if she was close enough; though she had to admit that Mrs Eldon had treated her better of late.

'I don't think Richard would want to be walking out with me. He has much more important friends.'

Thomas brightened. 'You don't think so?'

'No, Thomas, I don't think so.'

Heartened by this, Thomas gave her a less tentative kiss, though he felt it was not reciprocated in quite the same way.

Grace had the whole day free as it was Sunday and there were no guests staying at the inn. She went to the forge and stood outside. The heat from the fire could be felt even though she was some distance away. The fire glowed and Mr Vanns stood hammering a horseshoe into shape, and plunging it into the fire. withdrawing and hammering again. Grace liked strolling round the forge, studying the tools, admiring the workmanship of the items they were making, but Mr Vanns would not let her come near the fire. 'You must show fire respect,' he had often told her.

She stood silently, not wishing to disturb him.

'Hello, young Grace,' he said glancing up. 'You wanting Thomas.'

'Yes? I thought as it was a sunny day we could take one of these excursions from Tunbridge Station to the seaside. I've never seen the sea.'

Thomas came into the forge from the door of the house, his face lighting up when he saw her.

Grace said. 'Shall we go out somewhere today?'

'She wants to go on one of these excurtain trains,' his father said.

'Yes, I thought perhaps Folkestone,' she said. 'Richard told me that's where the line ends. He said, if you want to go to Hastings, you have to change at a place called Ashford and that would probably cost more money.'

'How much will that be?' he asked embarrassed. He had no money of his own and relied on what his father chose to give him.

'A penny a mile, Richard said, but I don't know how many miles it is to Folkestone. Anyway I think I have enough money saved up. Let's at least go and find out.

'Is dat all right father?'

'Yes, off you go. I've only got to shoe Miss White's horse this morning, den I'll be free. I wouldn't mind going on one of dese excurtains myself; I could take your mother. We aint never seen the sea either.'

'Excursions, father, excursions.'

'Ex-cur-shuns,' he said carefully and laughed. 'I can't get my tongue round these new-fangled words I never heard afore. Go and ask your mother to make you up some food to take with you. Here, have this.' He dipped his hand in his pocket and shot some coppers and small silver coins into Thomas' hand.

'I'll go back and get something, too,' Grace said, 'then we can stay out all day.'

They turned as the clatter of horses' hooves was heard. Clarissa and Richard were outside. Mr Vanns ran out, taking his cap off as he went.

'Good morning, Miss White, Richard.'

'Good morning, Mr Vanns.' Richard dismounted and helped Clarissa.

'This is the horse I want shod today. Jakes told you, didn't he?' Clarissa said, pointing to Mountaineer. 'I shall return home on Richard's horse, which he will lead. Change the saddles Richard,' she ordered.

While he was doing so, Thomas and Grace emerged from the forge.

'Grace! How are you?' Richard said, delighted to see her. 'I missed you yesterday afternoon.'

Grace said, 'Thomas and I are going on an excursion train to Folkestone. We were just wondering how far it was. Do you know?'

'I'm not sure, about forty miles, I think.' He turned to Clarissa. 'Do you know?'

'How do you think I would know,' she snapped. 'Help me up now, Richard. We don't want to be late for luncheon.'

Annoyed at the way he was being spoken to, he deliberately stopped to whisper to Grace, 'Do you want some money?'

'Certainly not.' Grace tossed her head in the air,

Doubly chastened, Richard went over to Atlas and cupped his hands so Clarissa could mount. Today was not, nor was likely to be, a good one.

When they had gone Grace said, 'The fare should be about three and four pence at that rate.'

Thomas tipped the money his father had given him into Grace's hand. 'Here, you'd better have this. I'm sorry I haven't any more.'

'Never mind, Thomas. We'll put it with mine and you can pay the six and eightpence at the ticket office, I've got more money for the return fare.

Thomas and Grace marvelled at the speed they were travelling as the fields, trees and cottages sped by.

'How fast are we going?' Grace asked.

'About forty miles an hour I think.' He did not know, but had heard someone say that a few weeks ago. He was pleased that he could show Grace that he knew something she did not.

'What does that mean?'

'Well, if you travelled for an hour you would reach ...' but poor Thomas could not think of anywhere that was forty miles away. 'It's faster than a horse could travel,' he said, hoping that was a good enough explanation.

'If Richard said it was forty miles away, then we should be there in about an hour.'

Why could he not have worked that out. He wished he were clever like Grace. Why would she want to marry him?

At Folkestone they walked from the station to the sea, and sat on the stones. They were fascinated by the vast expanse of water that went as far as their eyes could see. There were many others on the beach who had been on the train. They were unwrapping the food they had brought and the children were laughing and squealing as they took off their shoes, hitched up their clothes and dipped their toes in the cold water. Grace said she could tell they were from London because she recognised the way they talked.

'I'm going to take off my boots and stockings and walk in the water,' Grace said.

'Be careful, you might be swept away. Look at those big waves coming.'

'If these waves, as you call them, are coming in, how can I be swept away?'

'I heard about a man who went into the water and he was sucked in and never seen again.'

She thought this a highly unlikely story and said, as she turned her back to him and slid the garters down and removed her boots and stockings. 'Well, you come with me then.'

But Thomas was not going to take his boots off. He thought the water might do him some harm. 'I'll come and stand nearby. Here, give me those.'

Grace walked slowly up and down because the stones dug into her feet. In a few places she could dig her toes in, enjoying the feel of sand on her feet. Then she splashed Thomas who was not pleased.

'Come on out now. I fancy something to eat,' he said.

Sitting down, Grace wiggled her toes and let them dry in the sunshine. She bit into a piece of pork pie and gazed out to sea. 'What's over there?' she asked pointing, 'Where the sea touches the sky?'

'France.' he said boldly, but he was not absolutely sure if this were true, but he did not want to sound ignorant, and he did know that France was close to England.

'Grace?' he said, after a moment's pause.

'Yes?'

'I want to ask you something.'

'What?' Grace was watching the seagulls flying overhead waiting for leftovers from their meal. When seagulls flew inland, she remembered her mother saying, it was a sign of bad weather to come.

'Will you marry me?'

'Marry you?' She laughed.

'I mean when you are old enough - or sometime.' Thomas did not mind when they were married as long as she married him.

Grace was taken aback. She knew he was keen on her, but marriage!

'You don't love me,' he stated, seeing her face with the tell-tale sign.

'You have taken me by surprise, that's all. I don't know whether I love you or not. I'm not sure I even want to be married.'

'Why not?' he asked, surprised. He thought the aim of all girls was to be married and have children.

'I haven't seen anything in marriage that's favourable. Look at Bridie Smith, she's twenty-five and looks forty, she has six children and another on the way and little money. I don't want that sort of life, not for me, nor my children.'

'But Willie Smith is a common labourer.' Thomas pulled back his shoulders. 'I'm a skilled man, or I will be soon when I finish my apprenticeship this year.'

'Let's leave it for now, shall we, Thomas? I like you very much and perhaps, one day, who knows.'

Thomas miserably began packing up the cloths and bags and stuffing them in his pockets. Grace took two apples from her bag, and they munched them as they walked along the water's edge..

'My lips taste sort of salty,' Grace said, licking them.

'That's cause the sea is full of salt, silly.'

'Is it really? I didn't know that.'

'Oh, hadn't Richard told you?'

While Thomas and Grace were on their way to the seaside, Richard was at luncheon with the Whites. When the meal had finished, Clarissa asked Richard to come into the parlour, as she wanted to discuss something with him. Richard wondered why it had to be the parlour, he had never liked the room on the few occasions he had been in it; too gloomy. The wallpaper was dark green and on two walls shelves full of books covered them. On a desk stood an oil lamp, and behind it a chair with wooden arms and leather seat and back. Although it was a masculine room, it was not to his taste and gave him a feeling of foreboding. Clarissa went behind the large desk and indicated that Richard should sit opposite. He felt as if he were being interviewed.

'I've been thinking about this for some time. I want to go into the brewing business.'

'Whatever for?'

'I've told you, because my father should have left his brewery to me. I could have run it. It's church on Sunday, visiting uninteresting people in the afternoons and absorbing knowledge I'm not in a position to act upon. I can't stand it.'

'But, Clarissa. It is so hard for women in commerce and you have no experience'.

'I know that, but it's not impossible. Anyway I *do* know how it's run, he used to tell me.'

'Telling you about a thing and actually doing it are two very different things.'

Though Richard was not amongst those who believed that women could not do as well as men, given the right education and circumstances, he knew it would be an uphill struggle. Men were far from ready to treat women as equals. In fact, he doubted if that day would ever come. But seeing she was not going to take any notice of what he was advising, he said, 'So, what are you intending?'

'First of all I'm going to see Mr Grieves at my father's brewery and see if I can buy it back.'

Richard was speechless, incredulous even, that she contemplated such a move, and was even more certain she would be disappointed.

'I shall consult my accountant and solicitor,' she went on, 'and get them to make an appointment for me to see Mr Grieves.'

'Is he the present owner?'

'Yes.'

'I hope you know what you're doing. I don't think you realise just what you're undertaking.'

The next week the appointment was made and Richard was summoned after work on Saturday to accompany Clarissa to her father's old brewery. A young lad took their horses from them when they arrived. They had to walk past the drayman who was turning the horses and cart around. Impatient to see Mr Grieves Clarissa hurried ahead but Richard took her arm and made her stand and wait as he thought she might get crushed. The hooves clattered on the cobbles, the oppressive aroma of malt filled the air and the throb of an engine seemed to shake the whole place.

Charles Grieves, dressed in the new fashionable shorter frock coat and black narrow trousers greeted them. He was almost as tall as Richard and had to bend low to accept Clarissa's hand.

'Miss White, how pleasant to see you. Are you and your mother quite well? What can I do for you? Your accountant was not very forthcoming.'

'Yes, thank you Mr Grieves. This is Richard Wakefield. I wonder if he could be shown round. Richard knows nothing about brewing. Is Latimer still here?'

Mr Grieves went to the door of the office. 'Get Latimer to show this gentleman around,' he shouted to a passing workman.

Richard waited outside the office until Latimer appeared, roughly dressed in a striped shirt, kerchief round his neck, coarse trousers tied under the knee, held up by braces and a wide leather belt.

'I'm Richard Wakefield.' He held out his hand, Henry Latimer stared at it before wiping his hand on the back of his trousers, and shaking it.

'I'm 'enry Latimer. You want to be showed around. This way, Sir.'

'How long have your worked here,' Richard asked, as he followed him. He had to raise his voice as the sound of the engine became louder.

'Twenty-four year next month.'

'Then you worked for Miss White's father?'

'I did.' He pushed a door open and went in. 'This is the milling room.' Bags of malted barley were stacked against the walls. 'This malt here has to be milled into fine particles, see.' The smell in the store was a dry malty one, and the air was filled with fine dust particles. They moved on and the boom of machinery became louder.

'This is the engine room,' he shouted. 'This powers the whole brewery.' He theatrically swept his hand in front of him. The great pistons went back and forth, back and forth, the steam hissing with every revolution, and Richard stared at the huge wheel cogs which fitted into one another as they turned and moved the pistons. He had no technical knowledge at all and was keen to find out the names of all the machine parts. What little he did know he had gleaned from the modern machinery displayed at the Great Exhibition.

'Very impressive,' Richard shouted back. 'What exactly does it drive?'

'Everything. It draws water from the well for one thing and it turns the grinder that you saw in the milling room.'

They moved into the area where there were two huge covered cast iron vats. These were being heated by steam coils. Richard began to sweat and wished he could remove his coat.

Latimer went on: 'The water has been drawn up and it's gone into these vats and been heated.' They walked over to another area where revolving rakes slowly stirred the mixture. 'The mashing process ...'

'Just a minute, what's mashing?'

Latimer gave him a glare as if to say he was just coming to that. 'Mashing involves mixing hot water from the tanks with crushed malt in the grist case. After two hours a sugary solution called wort is drained from the mash and is run into the copper. More hot liquor is sprayed over the grains at the bottom of the mash tun to get out all the remaining sugars.'

Richard peered into a tun where the left-over grains lay at the bottom. 'What do you do with this?'

'That's what we call draff and we sell it to local farmers for cattle feed.' Richard was fascinated. 'Now, all that I've shown you has been going on since around six-thirty this morning and this copper is full of wort. Now the hops are added and this is boiled to extract their bitterness.'

Richard watched as the men tipped in the hops. How interesting to see where the hops that he had picked eventually landed. The aroma was very pungent and the steam from the liquid swirled around them and was drawn up into the roof space to escape.

'Next?' Richard queried. He was rather enjoying himself as he had always had a quest for new knowledge which he usually acquired from books.

'The wort will be strained through a sieve and pumped away for cooling.' Latimer went on, still raising his voice. 'More liquor is added depending what strength is wanted and then yeast. The yeast converts the sugar in the wort to alcohol. It's called fermentation.'

'How long does this - what did you call it - fermentation take?'

'About seven days and ....'

There was a flurry of rustling skirts behind him. 'Come, Richard, we are leaving.' Clarissa swept past him, down some stairs and disappeared from sight.

'Thank you, Mr Latimer. I see I must go.'

At least he had learned something of interest but judging by the look on Clarissa's face, she had not.

'He was so - so condescending, almost laughed in my face.' Clarissa stormed out of the building and snapped her fingers at the boy to get their horses.

Richard said, 'I did warn you. Why should he sell his business? From what I could see, this brewery appears well run to me.'

'I should think so. My father left it in an extremely good state. I know because he told me.'

'You're being ....' Richard began.

Clarissa did not want to hear any more and went over to the steps to mount her horse. 'I don't care what you or Grieves say, I *am* resolved to get a brewery of my own.'

Richard mounted Atlas and as they rode side by side he said, 'Perhaps you could find a brewery that is run by a woman. Businesses that were run by men are often passed to their wives or daughters when they die.'

'I know that,' she snapped, thinking of her father. Then she frowned. 'That's not a bad idea.'

He wished he had not spoken.

Clarissa discovered that there was a widow, a Mrs Ellen Amoore, who ran the Eagle Brewery in Hastings. She sent a telegram informing her she and Richard were coming and they went down by train. Clarissa paid his fare, for which he was grateful, because she never seemed to realise the difference in his modest means compared to hers.

She asked a great many questions of the woman, and appeared satisfied with the answers given and what she had observed.

'See,' she said, as they returned to Tunbridge in their first class carriage, 'she can run her place without any problems, and I'm sure I can, too.'

'But she's been in the brewing business for years before her husband died. She did not have to start from the beginning. And did you notice her hands?'

Clarissa had, but she did not want to hear any objections. Her mind was made up. 'Why are you so negative? Have you no spirit of adventure?'

'I'm trying to be realistic.'

From that moment on Clarissa badgered her accountant and solicitor weekly to find what she wanted. She even had Richard deliver notes to them because, as she said, 'you work in the town'. It did not occur to her that he would have to walk the length of Bridge Street between his office and theirs. She went through the local papers as soon as they arrived, but it appeared nobody was selling a brewery. She was getting more frustrated by the day, and her mother, the servants and Richard bore the brunt of her displeasure.

However, one day a messenger brought a note to the house from her solicitor. Mr Bradstock had heard that there was a brewery on the Maidstone side of Hadlow whose owner had recently died. Though it was not advertised as up for sale, he had heard that the executors would need to dispose of it in the not too distant future. Clarissa could hardly contain her excitement and rode into Tunbridge immediately to find out more, passing the weary messenger on his way back.

'Miss White, I must warn you that I have only told you about this because you are so insistent, but I do not think it is a good business proposition. In fact I think it is a lost cause. It has been allowed to get run down and ....'

'Never mind that, I want to see it for myself, then I will make up my own mind. Can it be arranged for Saturday afternoon? I wish to take a friend with me.'

'Of course, Miss White, but please do not make any rash decisions without consulting me or Mr Manklow,' he pleaded, knowing full well his remarks would be ignored.

Childe's Brewery lay about a mile outside Hadlow. It was a small concern and Clarissa vaguely remembered her father mentioning a Mr Childe whom he had met at brewery functions.

Immediately they arrived Richard could see what a poor condition the place was in compared with the Eagle Brewery and Clarissa's father's. Before they even went inside, Richard was appalled at the state of the forecourt. Horse dung lay everywhere, many days old from the look of it, and the drayman's horse appeared in a poor state of health.

'Look at that.' He pointed in front of him as they dismounted. 'That will give you some idea of the state of this place.'

'That can soon be remedied,' she said.

A ferret-faced individual greeted them at his office door looking surprised to see Richard. 'My name's Jacob Lancing, I'm like, the acting manager. You're Miss White?'

'You assume correctly,' she said, disdainfully ignoring his proffered hand which was none too clean.

'I 'ad a message that you wanted to look round the brewery.' He grinned, showing blackened teeth.

Richard said, 'I would like to look at the books first, Mr Lancing.'

'Oh, well,' he said, uneasily. 'I aint had much time to do books, what with Mr Childe's being so ill, like. He used to do them, see.'

'Just show me what you have then.'

They went into the office and Richard had to remove papers from a chair so Clarissa could sit down. Lancing reached for two ledgers behind him and shoved the detritus on his desk to one side to push the books in front of Richard.

One glance at the ill-kept ledger and poor writing set another alarm bell ringing in his head. 'When is the end of your accounting year?'

'January.'

'So you are preparing the ledgers now for that time.'

'Well, no, as I told you, Mr Childe did the books.'

'But you must have orders and invoices and wage payments, do you not?'

Jacob Lancing shifted in his seat.

Tapping her fingers on the desk while Richard was asking questions, Clarissa said, 'I want to see around now, we can come back here later.'

While she was studiously ignoring the poor state of the brewery in her desire to acquire it, Richard was getting worried that she would. How could he dissuade her?

'Please don't go ahead with this venture,' he pleaded, as they were returning. 'You can see what it's like. I think it is past redemption and you will lose money, and gain nothing. Even I can see that and I'm not in commerce.'

They journeyed back in silence, Clarissa deep in thought, Richard deep in despair, as he knew she was going to go ahead, regardless of his objections.

In the middle of November 1852 the contract was signed, and the brewery was in Miss White's hands, the executors unable to believe their luck. Little did she realise she was the laughing stock of the area when it was known what she had done. There was much ribald laughter in the Bell and, on the occasions when Richard was in there, he also came in for not a little teasing.

'I suppose you're in on this,' Robert Mills said one evening.

Richard glowered. 'I just cannot get the woman to see that she is buying a pig in a poke.'

'Too much money and not enough sense, I expect,' Robert said.

He agreed, but said nothing. Grace came over and said in his ear that Thomas wanted to marry her in the summer next year. She wanted to see his reaction.

''Oh, oh,' he stuttered He had ignored the fact she was old enough to marry. 'You're awfully young. Couldn't you wait until the year after perhaps?'

'What difference would another year make? I'll still be a servant, only this time a married servant who can just about read.'

'That's why I want you to make something of yourself.'

'You know I can't do that, like Miss White knows she can't rescue that brewery. But she's got money and even if she loses some, there'll be more where that came from.'

Richard did not know what to say. In his opinion, she was too young to tie herself down, but who was he to say what she should or should not do. In truth, he did not want her to get married at all but could not reason why.

Richard wanted time to think so he strolled to Mr Cox's gardens. Hop-picking had long ceased, but he had heard that the gypsies had not moved away, but were picking apples. He came to the area where they were, and was greeted with muted pleasure - the gypsies were not given to overblown gestures. Lunia's little daughter, Centine, ran up to him and started jabbering away in Roma. As usual, he could not understand what she was saying.

John Hern came up and greeted him. 'It's good to see you again. You're not picking any more, Fanny told us.'

'No, I have a job in an accountant's office in Tunbridge. I have also bought a cottage in Three Elm Lane.'

'Yes, Samuel told me that was what you were going to do.' Richard was expecting the usual comment on his age, but John said, 'We are expecting another child soon.'

'That's wonderful. Another grandchild for Charlotte and Samuel. I expect they are pleased.'

John nodded, and said, 'I must return to work.'

'Do you prefer fruit-picking to hops?'

'They're both work.'

They each gave the other a wry smile and shook hands again and Richard walked on towards Hartlake Bridge.

When he reached the narrow bridge he peered over the wooden palisade. The water was flowing fast but this year, so far, the Medway had not flooded. In fact, it was drier than the previous year when he had been picking. He watched as a barge was being manhandled along the bank towards Maidstone, marvelling at the strength of the man.

Tomorrow, on his Sunday off, he would have to examine the books he had brought home. He was not relishing it.

'Clarissa, I have to say it, this brewery is in an even worse condition than I first thought. It is my opinion that Jacob Lancing has been embezelling. I cannot make head nor tail of the invoices. I cannot see when or if they have been paid, and when you go to the bank tomorrow, I think you will find there is little money in the account. Neither can I see many orders to be fulfilled. It is just as well you got this place for next to nothing because if, and I emphasise if, you hope to make a go of it, you are going to have to pour in a great deal of money.'

'I'm sure you are exaggerating.'

'No, I am not,' he said forcefully. How could he make the woman see what she had done? 'I shall have to tackle Lancing and see if I can pin him down. And I certainly think he should be sacked.'

'We can't sack him, he's the only one who knows enough about the brewing system to keep it going.'

'In that case you shall have to keep him till you can get someone else who is competent - and that's not going to be easy. Who will want to work in a run down brewery?'

Clarissa was duly chastened. Richard could see she was beginning to realise just how foolhardy she had been. 'We'll just have to cope.'

'We? Don't you realise I already have a job?'

'What do you earn?' she asked.

He was taken aback. 'Surely that's a private matter.'

'Tell me. I'll give you more.'

'But I'm not competent enough to do what needs to be done. I am not a qualified accountant, though I can read a balance sheet. And, I know nothing about brewing, other than what I learned from Latimer. I can't help you, not sufficiently to get you out of this mess.'

'I'll give you twenty-two guineas. I'm sure that's more than you earn now.'

'It will not make me any more competent. No, Clarissa, you must look for someone else.'

She stamped her foot. 'I don't want anyone else. You are good enough. Twenty-three.'

'You'll be wasting even more money. Supposing it's not a success, I'll be out of a job and you'll have lost hundreds of pounds.'

'Please, Richard. I know you can do it,' she pleaded, an attribute she was not normally familiar with. 'You're the right person and I can get on with you. You understand me. Another person will not be the same and, as you said, who will want the job?'

He was in a quandary. He did not want to forsake her because she had been good to him, even if it were on her own terms. And as well as being taught to ride, he had learned a great deal from her.

'I'll buy you a horse,' she said in desperation.

CHAPTER 9

The money Richard had been offered he could hardly refuse, though he was still worried about his ability to deal with the uphill struggle ahead of them. If the condition of this brewery was as dire as he thought, the whole project could fail. Clarissa could go on her way receiving her income, even if she had lost money. He would have nothing. He could not imagine Clarissa supporting him till he found another position.

The ledgers had now been prepared well enough to go to an accountant, at least he hoped so. Richard asked Clarissa to get Mr Manklow to take on the audit, because he thought the one Mr Childe had appointed was as incompetent as Jacob Lancing. The firm was definitely in deficit, but how badly Richard had difficulty in estimating though he thought it amounted to hundreds.

When he tackled Lancing about the orders and invoices, he said he did his best when Mr Childe became ill, but he was not good at figures. Richard could well see that, but there seemed to be no attempt to keep them properly, if at all. He told Clarissa that he wondered if the accountant was in league with Lancing. Richard could not believe that a responsible firm would have let the business get into that position without some supervision.

At the first opportunity, Richard asked Clarissa to dismiss Jacob Lancing. There was much blustering about how they could not manage without him, and how he had kept the brewery going without any help. However, Richard informed him in no uncertain terms what he suspected. Lancing tried to wriggle out of it, but realising that he could be prosecuted, he stormed out saying, 'This place aint never going to succeed and if Miss White thinks as how she can make it pay, she's mistaken. It wasn't in a good condition even when Mr Childe's was there. You just wait and see if I aint right.'

Unfortunately, Richard thought he could well be.

With the knowledge he had gained from the other brewery, Richard tried to discover precisely how the brewing process was carried out at Childe's, but Lancing had been very secretive, and the men reluctant to speak to him. However, one of them, Josiah Smith, asked if he could take Lancing's place after he left. Clarissa was not keen, having judged the man unsuitable because she did not like the way he dressed, or spoke to her. Richard prevailed upon her to see past these things. The man knew more about it than anyone else there. Richard thought him to be a man he would be able to communicate with, and so learn more for himself.

One piece of good fortune, amongst the gloom, was finding a man to be the bookkeeper. Mark Littlejohn interviewed well and was eager. Richard advised Clarissa to appoint him and hoped that Mark would justify his faith in him. Richard went to a great deal of trouble to impress upon him the dire position that the business was in, and that they would not be able to pay what he might earn somewhere else. But he said he understood and that it was a challenge. Richard wondered if he would still be saying that when he actually went through the ledgers, but he had the air of a man who was ambitious and would go far, and was of a mind to wait.

One thing Clarissa insisted upon was that the wages were reduced. Richard was reluctant to do this as the men's co-operation was needed, but he could see her argument. He had discovered that they were being paid three pence a week more than other breweries were paying their men. This, no doubt, was Lancing's doing as a form of keeping the men quiet over his devious machinations. It was this that had to be dealt with the next morning.

The horse Clarissa had bought for Richard she called Chanticleer, and at six each morning Richard walked the mile and a half to her stable before they set off together. He had to admit that Clarissa did not shirk going to the brewery daily, and she did listen to what Richard put forward. He knew that she now realised, reluctantly, just how deeply she would have to dip into her pocket, with no guarantee that she would ever succeed.

Richard gathered most of the men together, leaving those preoccupied with the process that had started that morning to speak to later.

'I don't have to tell you that this brewery is unprofitable, I think you must have realised that. Miss White has already put, and will have to go on putting, a great deal of money into it in order to try to bring it into profit. This is not going to happen overnight. However, I am sorry to have to tell you that you will have to take a cut in wages.'

There was much grumbling and one man muttered loudly, 'Look at dat dress, dat would cover my wife and der kids in clothes for a year.' Another said, 'It's all very well for 'er,'

Clarissa was about to protest, but Richard nudged her to keep quiet. 'You may not have realised it but Mr Lancing gave you a rise of three pence a week which he was not in a position to do.'

'But we got used to it now. We can do a lot with thrupence.' said one.

'Yeah, buy three eggs for a start.'

'Or - or - a quarter of cheese, I reckon,' said another, not quite sure as he did no shopping.

'I know, I know, but if we do not succeed, you will have no money, because you will have no job.' Richard let this sink in. 'Mr Lancing did not do the business any good; no good at all. You must see that.'

One man stepped forward while the men still muttered angrily amongst themselves. Richard had had his eye on him as a promising candidate for promotion at some time in the future.

'Yes, Harry.'

'If we do as Miss White asks, will we have it back in the future?'

'Yes, I guarantee that if we succeed, you will benefit. Isn't that correct, Miss White?'

Clarissa was speechless but, having been put on the spot as Richard intended, she agreed with a slight nod of her head.

'That did not go too badly, much better than I thought.' Richard sat back in the chair of Clarissa's office and stretched his legs in front of him. 'I was not looking forward to that.'

She went behind her desk. Now that a bookkeeper had been appointed, Richard was a refugee. He would have to get her to buy a desk so he could share an office with Littlejohn.

'And I am not looking forward to paying out more money on your promises.'

'I know that, but I think you owe the men something if you get their co-operation.'

'I don't owe them anything.'

Richard let that go as he was in no mood for confrontation. He wanted to bring up something in the future which would be much more controversial.

He said, 'I have to get more business and I really don't know how to go about it. What did your father do?

Much to his surprise Clarissa said, 'I don't know exactly.'

'But you told me that you knew everything there was to know about his brewery.'

'Well, I do not.'

Richard suppressed a wry smile, but could not help observing, 'Not as easy as you thought, is it?'

She pursed her lips.

As they rode home side by side, Richard said, 'The order books show that there are only a few beer houses still taking beer from us and at the rate we're going, they will not be ordering any more. I'm not even sure of the quality we are producing, probably not that good. I shall have to talk to Josiah about it. He has shown me what goes on in more detail, but I still don't know enough. Perhaps I shall have to go around all the hostelries, inns and beer houses and spy on them.'

'Will you be any good at it?'

'I shall have to be, won't I?'

Richard had just walked from Clarissa's. It was Saturday, a bitterly cold March afternoon, the first Saturday afternoon he had had free for weeks. He had just slumped in his armchair wearily contemplating preparing a meal, when Grace let herself in.

'Why, Grace,' he said, jumping up, pleased to see her. 'I haven't seen you for weeks. How are you?'

'All right. I couldn't come this morning like usual - when you're not here.'

'You seem to have grown some more since I last saw you.'

'Have I? What shall I do? Same as usual?'

'Yes, it always looks so tidy when I get home. I have been working all day on

Saturdays since Miss White bought the brewery, and most Sundays here.'

'Good.' She went through to the kitchen to get her brushes.

'Grace. You wouldn't get me something to eat, would you? Before you start?'

She put down the brush and dustpan. 'What do you want?'

He studied her closed face. 'You don't seem very happy. Have I upset you? Did I forget to leave you your money? You must tell me if I do. I have been so occupied with ...'

'No, money's been there. What do you want to eat?'

'Don't bother, Grace, I'll get something. You need to get on.'

Richard went into the pantry and brought out two eggs. He filled a saucepan with water from the pail and took it to the range. He stood waiting while Grace riddled the fire and took out the ashes from underneath.

'Won't be very hot yet as the fire's low. I'll get some coal and wood,' she said.

'I'll get them.' As he came back it dawned on him why she was so miserable.

'I haven't taken you to Tunbridge Wells, is that why you are upset?'

'You have been too busy, you just said.'

'Oh Grace, I am so sorry. I have been busy, but I shouldn't have forgotten my promise. Will you forgive me?'

Ignoring him, Grace pulled the carpet away from the fender, rolled it and dragged it outside. From the scullery he watched her attack the carpet vigorously as it hung over the line. Richard recalled this same scene last year.

'When you have finished and I've eaten, shall we look in the newspaper and see if there's a concert on at the Assembly Rooms?' Still receiving no reply, he worked on the assumption they would do so.

While eating his boiled eggs and bread, he spread the paper on the table before him. 'Look, next Saturday afternoon there's something. Can you get the time off? Shall I ask Mrs Eldon? Tell her it's a special occasion.'

'It depends who's staying, special occasion or not.'

'I'm sure she'll let you go. After all, you come here on a Saturday.'

'But I'm not here for long, am I? And I can shift the day or the hours even, like I did today.'

'All right Grace. Leave it for me to sort out. You do still want to go to Tunbridge Wells to a concert, don't you?'

'Yes,' she said, barely audibly.

Back at the Bell, Grace asked if she could fetch the dress, which had been kept in a chest in Mrs Eldon's bedroom since the evening it was given to her. She stood now in her own room staring at it as it lay on her bed. Her eyes filled, making the dress a blurred mass of green. Did she want to go to Tunbridge Wells, or to a concert? She did not know exactly what a concert was - people singing and playing things she had been told. James played the fiddle and they all sang in the Bell, but it must be better than that. What she had wanted more than anything else last year was to go out with Richard, and to show off the dress that she had always desired. But, as he said, she had grown. So, if she had grown, did he not realise it would no longer fit her? Silly, stupid girl, to want to make life better for herself, but a silk dress was not going to do it.

That evening, she asked Thomas to walk with her to Richard's cottage where she pushed a note under the door saying she no longer wished to go anywhere with him. As they walked back to the Bell she told Thomas that she would marry him in the summer.

Richard seldom drank at John Eldon's nowadays. He no longer had to hire his horse, and he could get to Clarissa's along footpaths without passing the inn. But he wanted to wish Grace a happy birthday.

The tap room was the same as usual, the older men in their smocks, smoking their clay pipes and reminiscing. The younger ones in their more modern, but shabby, working clothes were in the newer part of the Bell and the middle-aged not quite sure where they wanted to drink. They all greeted Richard in a friendly manner, enquiring about the brewery and marvelling at how it was still managing to survive.

Grace brought him his usual drink, and he caught her hand as she moved away.

'Don't go, Grace. I was sorry to get your note. I have hurt you, haven't I?'

'We are no longer the same.'

'What do you mean?'

'I'm a servant, you're an important man of business.'

'But Grace, I - I -.' But he realised what she said was the truth. He was moving away from his class, but he did not want to lose her. Lose her what? Her friendship? But he saw what she meant, she was not his friend, she was his servant.

'I want to wish you a happy birthday and I have bought this for you.' He gave her a box. In it was an ornament of a lady in a green crinoline dress, wearing a hat with pink roses round it, and carrying a little dog under her arm. He thought she would like it for her room. He waited for her to open it, to see her pleasure like he had with the dress.

'I shall look at it later,' she said, tucking it into a pocket and moving away. She turned back. 'A happy birthday to you too. I have nothing for you this year as I am saving up to get married.'

'That's - that's wonderful, Grace,' he said, trying to sound as though it did not matter. 'What date?'

'In August, we think. It's not fixed yet. We have to find somewhere to live first and get some furniture.'

'You will tell me so I can buy a wedding present for you, won't you?'

Grace nodded and went behind the long table in the newer part of the inn, where she was given birthday wishes by some of the younger men. Richard's birthday had been forgotten.

Thomas and Grace found two rooms in Widow Fletcher's house not far from the Bell. Today, bright with late spring sunshine they went into Tunbridge on market day to look around for second hand furniture.

'Look, Thomas, there's a nice table, and two chairs to go with it.'

'It looks a bit rickety,' he said, leaning on a corner.

Grace was disappointed. She thought the chairs had pretty backs, She did not argue, she wanted Thomas to feel he was in charge. She had noticed how his strong, calloused hands were shaking.

They moved to another part where a man was trying to sell all his possessions. He explained that he was going to Australia in September, so he thought he would get rid of everything, find somewhere to rent till his ship sailed. When he arrived there, he could buy all new stuff. He was hoping to make his fortune from all the gold they had found there. Most of his furniture was well made but was showing signs of its age.

'I think this bed will be all right,' Thomas said boldly. Grace blushed as she studied the bed head and foot, which were leaning against a wall with the iron bed frame beside it.

'If you think so, Thomas.'

'What do you want for it?' he asked the man.

'It was two pound ten shillings when it was new, that was with the mattress. How about a guinea?'

'A guinea!' Thomas exclaimed, he had no idea it would cost so much.

Grace said, 'Would you accept fifteen shillings. We shall have to buy a mattress, you see.'

The man looked doubtful, though whether he was truly worried or just acting Grace was not sure, but she did not see why she should help pay for his passage.

'Come on, Thomas, we'll look somewhere else,' she said, walking away.

'Just a minute, just a minute, how about sixteen?'

She whispered in Thomas' ear, 'I don't think we'll get it for less than that; say yes.'

They did quite well at the market and beside the bed they found a cupboard, an oak chest, a table and two chairs which did not match the table, but were in good order.

'We'll have to ask Elias if he will take them back for us,' said Grace. 'I saw him at the horse wash just now, let's go and ask him. Let's hope he's returning empty. He might take us as well. I don't suppose he'll charge more than fourpence.'

'Fourpence!' Poor Thomas was trying to take in just how expensive getting married was going to be. With no money of his own, he had never had to manage it, unlike Grace.

'I bet you're pleased you're getting married,' Susan said, as they stood in Grace's small bedroom.

'Yes.'

'You don't sound very excited, I'd love to get married to get away from dat old witch Clarissa White.

'Don't you like her?'

'Tell you the truth, since she bought dat old brewery, I don't see so much of her, thank goodness. She likes to boss you around too much for my liking. Tell you what though, Mrs White is much happier now her daughter's away so much. 'Orrible she was to 'er mother.'

'Let's look at my dress, I know it doesn't fit, but I might be able to do something with it.'

'All right, put it over your 'ead.' As Grace stood before her, Susan said, 'yes, I see what you mean. The length don't matter, but I can't do up dese buttons.'

'I thought I'd go to that dressmaker in Three Elm Lane, Miss Bridger. See if she can let it out, or suggest something else to make it fit.'

'Wouldn't you like a new dress? The Queen got married in white so I was told, wouldn't you like to get married in white?'

'There's nothing wrong with this dress. Anyway, we're saving up. Thomas doesn't earn money until he finishes his apprenticeship later in the year, and my few shillings won't go far, and I shall only get some of my meals now. Life's not going to be easy. Then when the children come....'

'I was telling Mrs White 'bout your wedding and she said she would find me something nice to wear. I don't know how she's going to do dat. I hope she won't forget, otherwise I've only got the two black dresses I work in.'

'That'll be nice,' Grace said, barely taking in what she was being told.

Childe's Brewery had made a small profit; a very, very small miraculous profit. Everyone breathed a huge sigh of relief from Clarissa and Richard at the top, to the twelve year old who had only been with them for four weeks and thought it must be something good if everyone was so happy. This profit did not, however, take into account the money Clarissa had poured into it.

'I think you must give the men a rise as you promised,' Richard said.

'As you promised, you mean.'

'Well yes. Even if it's only a penny, it shows you are considering them and you get the best out of them.'

'Your ideas are too radical for my liking. You'll be wanting to form a union next, like those men in Dorset. Fat lot of good it did them.'

'Strange you should say that, but it was the thing I was going to bring up a few weeks ago but did not get round to it.'

'No, no, no!'

'Hear me out, Clarissa. I just want them to put by a penny a week, and then if one of them falls on bad times, illness, say, then they can have a little money to tide them over.' He did not tell her that if he knew of any man who was in trouble, he gave a little out of his own pocket.

'The next thing you will want is for me to put money in, too.'

'That seems a good idea, I hadn't thought of that.'

'The answer is still no. Why, the men will then pretend they are ill to have a day off.'

'I would not let that happen.'

'No, that's my final word. Please do not bring this ridiculous matter up again.'

Grace knocked on the door of Elizabeth Bridger's and was ushered in. The cottage was of a similar design to Richard's but this main room was a sea of fabric and cloth. The floor was covered in pins, bits of cotton and off cuts of material of sundry types and hues. She wondered a spark from the fire had not set the place ablaze before now and Grace's fingers itched to clear it up.

'How can I help you, young lady,' she said, pushing her spectacles further up her nose.

'I have this dress,' Grace said, unwrapping the brown paper and lifting it out, 'but it's too small.' She held it against herself.

'Yes, I see. Put it on and I'll see what I can do.'

Grace took off her grey calico and put the dress on. Miss Bridger did up the buttons and walked around her saying, 'um, lift your arms, um, put them down, um, yes. Did I make this dress? It looks like my work.'

'I don't know, it was given to me as a present.'

'Was it a young man with an older woman.'

Mrs Eldon must have gone with Richard to describe her measurements. 'Yes. I've had it a year but have never worn it, and now it doesn't fit.'

Miss Bridger bustled over to a corner where, on top of a low cupboard, materials and other pieces folded haphazardly, lay in crazy confusion. With little care, she tossed bales aside and rooted around until she came across a length of cardboard that had a small amount of silk wrapped around it. 'Ah, here it is,' she said, triumphantly, taking it over to Grace. 'I thought I had some left.' She walked around her once more. 'I can put in a piece under the arm each side. Um, yes, I can do that. Let out a dart. Do you want a piece on the bottom to make it a bit longer, I might have enough.'

'No I'm not worried about the length, I haven't grown that much taller, I've just filled out a bit. What will it cost? Not too much I hope, because I'm getting married next week and we're saving.'

'That's lovely, my dear. Are you marrying someone in Golden Green?'

'Yes, the blacksmith's son.'

'Ah, young Thomas Vanns. I used to be friendly with his father, you know.'

Grace was not quite sure what was meant by this, but she did not pursue the matter, she was more anxious to find out the cost of the alteration.

'One and six, and I'll have it done the day after tomorrow. With more daylight in the summer, I can sew for more hours. I can't sew by candlelight for long because it hurts my eyes.'

'Thank you, Miss Bridger. I'll call by on Monday.' She left the cottage and went on to Richard's, hoping he would not be at home before she had finished tidying up.

CHAPTER 10

'Grace has got to see the Reverend Monypenny today.'

'Why's that then, Thomas?' his mother said as she ladled out the breakfast porridge.'

'Because she's not been baptised or confirmed, and he won't marry us else.'

'Is that so? No, don't suppose that good-for-nothing Brandon had time for that. Do they do the two together then?'

'I suppose so,' Thomas said, 'I'll find out later.'

Mr Vanns said, 'Looking forward to celebrating on Friday night?'

'What's this?' said his mother sharply.

'I'm only going for a little while. The lads said they'd buy me a drink.'

'Now, you watch how much you're drinking. Grace won't want you in church disgracing yourself on her big day, breathing beer fumes all over her.

'Oh, leave 'im alone, he's only going to get married once.'

'You keep an eye on him, d'you hear. Things can get out of hand. I've known you come home ….'

'Yes, yes. I'll look after him. Anyway, he's got to work in the morning 'afore the wedding. I can't manage all I've got to do by myself.' He winked at young Thomas. 'You enjoy yourself, son.'

Grace frowned. Thomas was surrounded by lads around his age who were plying him with ale. She told William Carey when he ordered more not to give too much to Thomas. 'Oh, he'll be all right. His father's looking out for him.'

From what Grace could see, someone needed to keep an eye on his father. Though it was embarrassing, she even whispered in Thomas' ear to go easy, but he was too merry to care what she said, and laughed inanely and tried to give her a kiss. Not wishing to be thought a nag, she said no more.

In her room, Grace and Susan were preparing for the wedding that afternoon. She wondered if she would see Richard there. She had left him a note last week saying the time.

'You look lovely, Grace. And that brooch is so pretty.'

'Mr and Mrs Eldon gave me that last year.'

'You are lucky. Miss White aint never given me nothing, only paid for my dresses, apron and caps. She even told me I was lucky she did that 'cause she knew of some 'ouses where the servants had the money taken out deir wages.'

'That's class for you,' Grace said, bitterly. 'What they've got they make sure they keep, and if they can get more money by exploiting people, so much the better.'

'What's exploiting mean?'

'Taking advantage. Like Miss White does of you.'

'Yeah.' Susan agreed, still not sure what Grace meant. There was always rich people and poor people, that was just the way things were.

'Mrs White did find you something then, Susan. That dress looks nice on you.'

Susan held out the skirt of the white muslin dress with sprigs of blue flowers and green leaves dotted over it. 'I don't know where she got it from. Maybe it was one of Miss White's when she was young.'

'I think you look very pretty,' Grace smiled.

'Oh, no. No. You look beautiful. Your hair is such a lovely colour, all goldy and shining. Not like mine which is mousy and dull.'

Grace looked up at the rectangle of glass high above her head.' It's very hot in here. I wish that window would open.'

'Is your friend Richard coming to de wedding? Did he buy you a present?'

'I don't know if he's coming, he just said he wanted to know when it was, so I presume he will.' In some ways Grace did not want Richard there. Why, she could not quite decide. He had been so good to her and he had paid for curtains and two sheets and a counterpane. Thomas was not keen on accepting his presents, but she said they needed all the presents and money they could get.

Mrs Eldon tapped on the door and came into the room. 'Here Grace, I thought you would like to wear this lace bonnet. It belonged to my mother, and I wore it at my wedding.'

'Thank you, Mrs Eldon. You are very kind, and have given me so many things for our home. I shall miss you.' Her eyes filled with tears.

'Now, now, Grace, this is your wedding day. You mustn't cry and you won't be leaving us altogether, will you?'

Grace nodded, and found a piece of rag in her drawer to dry her eyes.

Susan said, 'I've got to go back to see to Mrs White's luncheon now. When you walk by de house to St Mary's, I'll be waiting to join you. I expect there'll be quite a crowd of you.'

Mrs Eldon said, 'I'm sure there will - Grace is a very popular girl. Mr Eldon will be proud to be by her side.'

Grace sat on her bed when they had all gone. Would she be happy? Thomas was a kind man, she had no fears there. But did she love him or, as she had said at one time, did she love him enough? What she feared most was having a child every year like most women seemed to have. She did not dislike children, but she had seen so many worn out with childbearing and the subsequent poverty a large family endured. Blacksmiths might be skilled men, but they still did not earn a great deal of money. She stood up and fetched a brush from her drawer. Then there was Thomas' brother, Stephen, who would be starting his apprenticeship soon. When he had finished, that would be three ways the money would have to be divided, even though they would be taking on more work. Mrs Vanns was lucky only having two. Thomas had said something about her losing two babies soon after birth, and miscarriages. Surely there was some way that women could stop having so many children. Once she had been told that you could get rid of a baby before it was born, but she did not say how, and Grace did not like to think of doing something like that.

She reached for the lace cap and tried it on. No use worrying about it now. Wonder if Thomas is having similar thoughts to mine? She smiled - dear Thomas, he did love her.

Grace thought she heard a commotion outside, but having no window she could see through, she thought it must be her imagination.

Susan came rushing in. 'Oh, Grace, it's ter'ble, ter'ble.'

'What's terrible?'

'It's Thomas,' she said. 'He's been burned.'

Knowing Susan's inclination to exaggerate she said, 'That's a pity, but can't he be patched up? I'm sure whatever it is will soon be better.'

Mrs Eldon followed Susan into the room.

'What is it Mrs Eldon? You look dreadful. Are you feeling ill, can I get something for you? Sit down here.'

'No, I'm all right. It's – it's - there's been an accident.'

'Yes, Susan just said, but …'

'I think you'd better see for yourself. I've been told it's serious.'

As they neared the smithy the piercing screams, like the whistle of a locomotive, became louder and more harrowing to hear and Grace realised the gravity of the situation even before she reached the forge. Men were searching for wood to make a pallet on which to put Thomas. She could not see his injuries, but from the agonising cries, she knew he had been dreadfully hurt. What could have happened? As the men moved to one side to lift Thomas Grace glimpsed his face, or rather, what had once been his face. She let out a gasp and clasped her hand to her mouth. One side was a mass of blood and raw like meat on a butcher's chopping board. He had no eye that side. His left arm was burned and blistered from shoulder to claw-like fingers and his right hand was also burned a little. His shirt was blackened and sticking to his chest and most of his hair was singed away. Grace felt sick and wanted to rush to his side, but she could not move.

Mr Vanns stood numb with shock just inside the forge and his wife was crying uncontrollably. Someone had been to fetch Stephen, who had been having reading lessons. When he arrived Grace grabbed him and held him close. She walked him a few steps from the scene and his mother came over to them and sat him on a nearby tree stump to explain and Grace moved away. Mr Eldon came running from the inn which he had closed up.

Mrs Eldon and Susan had their arms around Grace as they watched some of the men, trying to occupy themselves, so they did not have to take in the enormity of the scene. Elias, the carrier was fetched, luckily not out on a job. They lifted the pallet up to place Thomas in the waggon. He shrieked at the movement, but his pain was so severe that he cried and screamed almost without let up.

A man asked if Mr Vanns wanted to go with Thomas. No response. The man repeated more loudly. 'Thomas, Thomas! Elias is going to go into Tunbridge to a doctor. Do you want to go?'

Thomas' father stared at the man with unseeing eyes, but his mother said they would and asked Grace to come too. Mrs Vanns looked around at the men and catching John's eye she asked if he would take care of Stephen because she did not want him to see his brother.

John put himself between the blacksmith and his wife and steered them towards the cart. Thomas was still crying out or moaning. John held out his hand to help Grace into the waggon and persuaded a reluctant Stephen, who was getting ready to go with them, to stay behind, explaining that his parents did not want to worry about him at the moment.

Stephen nodded, the tears running down his face, and Mrs Eldon and Susan took his hands as the sad procession moved off along Three Elm Lane towards the Hadlow road. The ruts were bone hard and the waggon dipped and swayed causing Thomas yet more pain, if such a position could be reached. He lost consciousness and his mother thought he had died but Grace, who was holding his least injured hand, assured her he was still breathing. Nearing the main road, they met Richard returning from the brewery. On seeing Grace in the carrier's waggon, he brought the horse to a stop. He removed his top hat.

'Grace, whatever's the matter. I was coming home to get ready...' He quickly took in the scene, the moans and intermittent screams, (he could not see the worst of the injuries) and the white-faced parents.

'Thomas fell into the fire at the forge,' Grace explained. 'We don't know how it happened yet. His father was there, but he cannot speak, he is ....'

'In shock, no doubt. What can I do?'

'I don't know.' She took her hands from Thomas's and bit her bottom lip. 'What can be done?'

'Shall I ride into town now and prepare the doctor? What doctor are you going to?'

'I don't know any doctors. Someone suggested a Dr Parker.'

'All right. I will go and find out where he lives and explain the situation.' He nodded to Grace and Mrs Vanns, saying, 'I am so sorry.'

Richard turned his horse and galloped into Tunbridge.

When Doctor Parker, forewarned by Richard, saw Thomas in the waggon before they brought him in to his room, he wondered how he had survived the accident, let along the journey. All he could do, he informed them, was to cover the burns with clean cotton cloths, and wait to see the outcome knowing from the extensive wounds that there was no hope. Thomas awoke from unconsciousness when they removed him from the waggon, and screamed when the doctor tried to touch him, but he slipped into a deep coma and died half an hour later.

Richard was waiting outside with the carrier, loathe to set off home in case he could be of further help. He and Elias were already of the opinion that Thomas would not survive, so when the sad trio came into the road, their fears were confirmed.

'Would you like me to take you home on my horse?' he asked Grace.

'No, I think I need to stay and comfort them.' She pointed to Thomas' grief-stricken parents. 'He has not spoken since the accident, so no one knows exactly what happened.' Grace broke down. 'Oh, Richard, how can they stand it? How shall I?' Tears ran down the side of her nose, past her lips and dropped on to her wedding dress where they mingled with some blood on the skirt.

Richard pulled her close. 'There, there, Grace. It's good to cry. That's what Mr Vanns needs to do. When you've seen to them, you are welcome to come to me if you want to talk. If you can't come this evening, perhaps tomorrow morning.'

The doctor and his assistant brought out Thomas' body, wrapped in a white sheet, and placed him in the waggon. The carrier called, 'Gidup, there,' and they moved off, Richard riding slowly behind.

Grace came to him very early the next morning. 'I couldn't sleep. I hope you don't mind.'

'I couldn't sleep either. I have been awake nearly all night thinking about you and Thomas. Have you had something to eat?'

'No, I left a note for Mrs Eldon saying where I had gone. She was very kind to me last evening. So was Mr Eldon. Oh, Richard, how am I going to get over this? I shall never forget his face - burned away - just raw - and the pain he must have suffered.' She started sobbing. 'I am glad he died. Is that ter'ble?'

'No, of course it isn't. He would have been in constant pain for months, years even, and so disfigured. I think he is with his Maker and at peace.'

Richard made breakfast for them both and she told him what had happened.

'It seems they could not get Thomas to wake up in the morning because he had had too much to drink.' She started crying again. 'I told him - I told him not to, and so had his mother before he went out *and* I told the lads as well. But men are so stupid. I hope they realise what they've done. It's all their fault.' She hurriedly wiped her cheeks with her fingers before going on. 'His father said Thomas *had* to get up and help him, which he did. Then it seems - it seems that Thomas, still half asleep, went to fetch a tool hanging on the wall, and as he stepped back he missed his footing. His father doesn't know what made him trip but he did, and couldn't get his balance and staggered headlong into the fire. He wouldn't have done that if he had not had too much to drink on Friday. He wouldn't, would he Richard? His father was so strict - so strict.' She put her head down on her arms and wept.

He went to her side, put his arms around her and held her tightly. He stroked her hair and let her weep till her sobs subsided.

'There, do you feel a little better? I will clear up these cups and plates, then we can talk about something less distressing. Sit in my armchair.'

On his return from the scullery, he pulled out a chair from under the table and sat opposite.

Grace spoke about her two rooms and what she would do with the furniture. 'I would like to keep the rooms, but half a crown a week is too much for me and I would have to spend money on food. I think I would be better staying with the Eldons, don't you? I can keep some of the furniture, that's if it will fit in my bedroom. Perhaps - do you think - could you take some - till I sort myself out?'

'Of course. I will do whatever I can to help you, don't worry about it ...'

So engrossed had Richard been that the knock on the door startled him. He opened it. 'Why, Clarissa!' He hit his forehead with his hand. 'Of course, it's Sunday. It completely left my memory. Come in. Grace is here.'

She swept into the room and glared at the girl sitting in Richard's armchair. Grace went to stand up.

'Stay there,' he said to Grace. He turned to Clarissa. 'You remember I told you I was going to Grace's wedding yesterday. Well, Thomas, her intended, had a dreadful accident at the forge. He was badly burned and died.' He indicated that Clarissa sit in the chair he had just vacated. She remained standing.

'How sad. Are you coming riding? We can both ride on my horse back to my house to fetch Chanticleer.'

'No, I don't think I can leave Grace just yet.'

Grace jumped up. 'Yes, you must go with Miss White. I will be all right now.'

'She does seem to have made herself comfortable here.'

'There is absolutely no reason why you should go. Sit down.' To Clarissa he said, 'I don't want to ride this morning, I am too distressed about the accident. Please excuse me. I will see you at the brewery tomorrow afternoon. I have to go to Cranbrook to the hop market first thing in the morning.'

Clarissa stamped her riding boot on the stone floor. 'I'm not used to being spoken to in such a manner, least of all for a servant. You will be expected for luncheon, as usual.' Without waiting for an answer, she left, slamming the front door behind her.

'You shouldn't have done that; she can make your life a misery. She has power, you haven't.'

'I don't like being told how to run my life. At work, that's different.'

Grace thought he was on uneasy ground and Miss White was not to be underestimated.

Heeding Grace's advice, he arrived for the Sunday meal, leaving Grace at the Bell on the way. No comment was made by either of them, but Mrs White glanced from one to the other knowing that there had been some difference of opinion between them.

'Did Clarissa tell you about the accident at the forge yesterday,' Richard asked.

'No. What happened?'

He explained.

'How dreadful; that must have been the wedding Susan was going to. I gave her one of your old dresses to wear.'

'You did what? How dare you?'

'I did not tell her it was yours. It was one you wore years and years ago. I doubt it would fit you. Anyway, it's a young person's dress.'

This added explanation did not alleviate Clarissa's mood. 'You still had no right, mother.'

Startlingly, Mrs White said, 'Oh, don't make such a fuss. The chances of her being able to wear it are very remote now the wedding's off.'

Clarissa was so astonished at her mother's outburst, she was silenced. Richard thought, bravo, Mrs White and winked at her.

But as Grace so shrewdly observed, Clarissa White was not one to be thwarted.

Hop picking was underway. The roads and lanes were crammed with gypsies, travellers and Londoners having their annual working break. Whenever Richard rode his horse past William Cox's farm he thought contentedly of his first time in Golden Green two years ago. What a lot had happened since then. He made a point of going to the Irish travellers one evening. He heard them singing round their camp fire while they ate their meal. They looked up as his horse approached.

'Well, look who's here everyone,' Dennis Collins said. 'We haven't seen you picking?'

'No. I work for a Miss White, she has bought a brewery and I am helping her get it on its feet.'

'Does the horse go with it?'

'It's not mine, but Miss White bought it for my use.'

'Too grand for us now,' said old Jeremiah with a grin.

'No, old chap. I do not think like that. You are all my friends.'

The widow, Catherine Clare, was some distance away, stirring a pot. She still looked sad. Her son sat close, as if afraid she would disappear like his father had done.

Richard jumped down from the horse. 'How is Catherine?' he asked softly.

'She finds it difficult, you know, not much money and her son to look after. And she and her husband were a devoted couple. His death was a terrible blow, so it was. Now, Sir, would you like to sup with us. There's plenty to go around.'

'That's very kind of you, I would be delighted. I have to cook for myself now I've left the Bell.'

Stew was ladled into a tin bowl and he sat cross-legged on the ground till it was dark. Chanticleer munched contentedly on the grass. About nine, he left them all singing Irish songs as the women washed the pots and pans.

He wanted to ride into Tudely in the hope of coming across the Leatherlands and Herns, but it was dark now. He made a note to see them at the weekend - perhaps after luncheon at the Whites. That is, if he was still going to be asked. The last week at the brewery had been fraught with tension and Clarissa made a point of going to Mark's office, where she would make sure that Richard would see her laughing with him. He could not be bothered playing such games. He gave Chanticleer a tap on his flanks and rode back to Clarissa's stable.

A ride and luncheon was taken the following week, though the atmosphere was still frosty between Richard and Clarissa. However, Mrs White was very communicative and he enjoyed conversing with her. Her daughter's daily absence at the brewery was obviously a relief to Mrs White and he found her quite entertaining.

It was the wettest October they had ever experienced, most of the locals agreed, and Richard could not remember it raining for so prolonged a time even when he lived in Clapham. Riding to and from the brewery was not a pleasant experience, and the only thing for which he was thankful was that he no longer had to walk there ankle deep in mud. The Medway was in flood, not an unusual occurrence, and some of the low-lying fields were already waterlogged and, he was told, Bridge Street in Tunbridge was all but impassable, which he could well imagine from his walk from the station. Today he had left the brewery before Clarissa and was stabling his horse before walking home. He went via the Bell, as it was a marginally less muddy than by the footpaths. He thought he might call on Grace to see how she was.

As he neared the inn, he met a small band of gypsies and enquired if the Leatherlands were in the area. He was told they were about to walk home from Mr Cox's. Richard removed his watch from his pocket. Yes, it was about the time they used to pack up. On impulse, he walked past the inn and went down the lane. About forty or fifty people were milling around Thompson's yard. Some of them were from the Irish shed, and the others were the gypsies that Richard had come to know when he had first come hop-picking. In addition, there were the Taylors whom he knew vaguely, having been told that they were relatives of the Leatherlands. The rest of the Taylor family were probably still hopping in Paddock Wood.

Sarah Taylor was holding a tiny child. Her son Thomas and daughter Emily were talking to each other. Little Centine clung to Lunia's skirt until she saw Richard and she ran up to him jabbering away as usual.

'My, how you have grown, little Centine. And I see you have a new baby sister.'

'Sas miri dia si O tikni chavvi. Come, see.' She grabbed his hand and pulled him over to her mother. Lunia's clothes were damp and the rain was dripping from her long black hair. She was clutching her baby close to her, trying to protect her from the drizzle.

'Hello. You will be glad to get out of this rain, Lunia,' he said. 'I saw Fanny last year and she told me you had a baby. How are you?'

John said, 'We are all well.'

'And Samuel and Charlotte?'

'They're over there.'

Richard looked to where John pointed. 'So they are. Are you walking back now?'

'No,' John Hern said, 'we're waiting for Mr Waghorne to bring the waggon back. Mr Cox thought it was too wet near the river to walk to Tudely. The road is covered to about a foot or eighteen inches on either side the waggoner told us, so that's why Mr Cox said we needn't walk. He's already taken the home dwellers and we're waiting until - ah, here it comes.'

The waggon drew up and John Waghorne jumped off. 'You'd certainly have been soaked if you'd walked,' he said to the assembled folk. 'Jump in now and we'll be off. You'll be glad to get into some dry clothes.'

'Sure, and we will that,' murmured Dennis Collins, as he pulled off his cap and scratched the top of his head.

Richard waved to them all and held little Centine's cold, wet hand, before handing her up to John. 'Bye, bye, Centine.'

He nodded his head at his gypsy friends. 'See you next year, I hope.' He gave a special smile and a wink to Fanny, even though he knew it might annoy her father if he noticed. Who knows what might have been had Fanny not been a Romany.

Centine said 'Kushti rarti', which Richard took to mean goodbye in her language, and waved her tiny hand. He waved back and watched as they climbed into the large blue and red waggon with the big wheels at the back. There were so many of them standing around, he could not imagine how they would all fit in. Most of Samuel's tribe were there – all the Leatherland family, with John, Lunia and their children, and the Taylors. There was a Henry Knight and his daughter, Will Diplock and several others he did not recognise. Last into the waggon were most of the Irish travellers he had spoken to from time to time.

'Squash up all of you,' the waggoner said, laughing.

'If I could ride on the hind horse, that'll make a bit more room, waggoner,' said a gypsy unfamiliar to Richard.

'By all means.'

'Want a leg up?' Richard went over to help. The waggoner took the reins of the first horse and shouting 'Gidup' he led the horse out of the yard and along the lane towards Tudely.

Richard waved again and watched as they disappeared out of sight round a bend. He turned towards Golden Green, anxious to get out of the rain.

He had hardly reached the front door of the Bell when he thought he heard a distant cry. He stood still, his head cocked. What could it be? He shouted. 'Mr Eldon, Mrs Eldon. Come here quickly. What do you think that sound is?'

John Eldon came running from the garden behind the stables alarmed at the sound of Richard's voice. Mrs Eldon came from the kitchen, followed by Grace. 'What is it, what's wrong?' John asked.

'Ssh. Listen.'

'I can't hear anything,' Grace said.

'Ssh, there are cries and shouts. Someone's in trouble. Listen.'

They stood silently at the front of the inn. Men and women on their way home from work also stopped, aware that something untoward was happening.

'Sounds like it,' John agreed. 'Let's go and see? They might need help.'

John and Richard left the inn and hurried down Hartlake Road, joined by others curious as to the sounds they could hear. As they progressed so the cries became clearer - wretched shouts, anguished howling and a horse whinnying in distress.

'It could be something to do with the waggon I saw off. Maybe it's got trapped in all that water,' Richard gasped as he ran beside John, 'and that bridge is very narrow.'

'Yes, I know, only about nine or ten feet I should think,' John Eldon said breathlessly. 'People have moaned about it for years on and off.'

As they sped along others joined them, alarmed at the cries.

CHAPTER 11

Thursday, 20 October, late evening/early hours of Friday morning
One horse was standing, with its hooves beneath lapping water and part of its harness trailing. How it had managed to climb out was a miracle. The other horse, its slipping feet hindering its rescue, was being hauled up the bank by the waggoner and another man. The waggon, tossing in the fast flowing waters, was disappearing in the fading light. The pole puller, was holding one woman clinging to the horse's harness. Richard recognised Fanny. He rushed to her over the broken bridge and put his coat about her shoulders.

'What happened - what happened Fanny?' She was shaking and he held her arm.

'We fell out of the w-waggon, it t-tipped over. I clung to something – a bit of the waggon I think, and then the gris was struggling beside me and …. Where are the rest of them, where are they? My parents, my sisters….' To herself, in Roma, she murmured, 'Latch lende, latch lende. - find them, please find them.'.

'I will look for them. See if you can get someone to take you to a house or the Bell.' Richard looked about him and saw Mr Cox standing dazed. 'Can you look after Fanny? I want to help the others. Don't worry Fanny, I'll find them,' he shouted above the roar of the river and shrill cries and commotion caused by the rescuers.

Mr Cox shook himself out of his daze and took Fanny's arm. 'Send anyone else you rescue to me,' he said, as he led her away.

Dusk had now given away to darkness. Richard tried to ascertain who had not been thrown in the water, or had been pulled out. He recognised John Lawrence, Mr Cox's bailiff, John Waghorne and Will Diplock. Henry, one of the Irish he had met a few days ago, was standing stiffly beside Richard, tears falling from his eyes, unable to move. Richard remembered his daughter telling him that she was a bit squashed. Richard could not see her.

'Selina, my Selina?' Henry kept saying. 'Where are you, my little one?'

Someone on the other bank called, 'Here, here.'

They all ran to see a body being hauled out, but whether alive or dead, Richard could not see. He knew that the chance of any survivors in the tumult of the swift water was very small but he had promised Fanny he would search for her family and search he would.

Other rescuers, some on the Tudely bank, were farther down the river from the bridge as they had seen the bodies had been swept that way. Most of the rescued men estimated that about ten had not been drowned. Apart from the waggoner, Henry Knight, the bailiff and Fanny, Richard was not sure who they were. At least two of the Irishmen, shocked and shivering in the October dusk, had been persuaded to go to Thompson's Farm by one of Mr Cox's hands, though they wanted to stay.

At midnight, a shout went up. 'Come here. Here, this looks like a body,' a man pointed. 'Here in this eddy. Has anyone a lantern?'

Someone shouted for a man with a lighted branch and beckoned him to come nearer. Arms reached down and grabbed a handful of clothing and the body was dragged out of the water and across to drier land.

Richard recognised Charlotte Leatherland. His eyes filled with tears and mingled with the mud on his face. 'Poor, poor Fanny,' he muttered to himself. 'Who else from your family are lost?'

'There's another one here,' a man shouted.

They crowded round as the second body was pulled from the water. It was Norah Donovan. Her long auburn hair was twisted round her face and neck; her eyes open, her clothes intact, but covered in weed that formed a pattern on her dress.

Friday, 21 October

Richard thought it must be around three in the morning. It was pitch black and fruitless to continue with the search, though hundreds, it seemed, stayed, unwilling to leave the bodies of their friends and loved ones to the furious, raging Medway. The few who had lanterns were farther down the river towards East Lock and beyond. News had spread so unbelievably fast and gypsies riding on donkeys came from all around - Barnes Street, Paddock Wood, Capel, Tudely, East Farleigh.

Richard went to Thompson's Farm on his way home. Though it was the middle of the night, he had to see how Fanny was coping. Mr Cox said she was sleeping restlessly and his wife was looking after her, and others that had been involved.

'I fear,' said Richard, 'there will be few of her family alive. I think all that have been saved, are all that will be saved. Her mother's body has been found. Perhaps you would tell her, and that I will see her in the morning. I am sure the rest of her tribe will take care of her. There are many gypsies arriving from neighbouring farms - to see their distress is too much to bear.'

Richard trudged disconsolately towards Three Elm Lane and home. Someone touched him on the shoulder and John Eldon, whom he had not encountered since they first arrived at the bridge, said, 'Richard, is that you? It is so dark, I can recognise no one.'

'What a dreadful night it has been, John. I am so weary I felt I had to get home for some rest, even though I wanted to go on searching.'

'Yes, I feel the same. I am going to offer the stables to house the bodies. I expect there will be an inquest soon, but I am not sure where that will be held, someone in authority will no doubt tell me.'

They continued their homeward journey, silent, reluctant to talk, almost too tired to think. People pushed past them rushing to see what had happened as word had spread. Richard said, forlornly, 'There is no hope of finding anyone alive, is there?'

'I fear not. The river is a raging torrent, I don't think I have seen or heard it so violent. No one could survive that.'

'No, no.' Why had he asked such a stupid question when he knew the answer? They reached Three Elm Lane.

'Well, goodbye John. When I have rested I will rejoin the search.'

'Mind how you go, you must not make yourself ill. You sound as if you are developing a cough.'

Strangely, no more bodies were found during the day on Friday, even though many, including Richard, stayed until dusk, poking the eddies with long poles, searching the banks, climbing dangerously along overhanging branches to peer into the raging river. Others were trying to console relatives awaiting news.

Saturday, 22 October

On Saturday, Richard was awoken early from a troubled sleep by a loud banging at the door. Hastily grabbing a gown, he stumbled down the winding wooden stairs and crossed the room to open the front door. He found Clarissa, crop in hand, mounted on her horse, glaring down at him.

'Where were you yesterday? And what are you doing still abed this morning?'

'Haven't you heard about the accident?'

'What accident? I've seen people crowding the lane and rushing about like idiots.'

'At the bridge on the way to Tudely. A waggon tipped over and many people are drowned, some of them my friends.'

'And you have missed coming to the brewery - for what reason. may I ask?'

'I was searching for bodies.'

'Couldn't others do that? It is not your job. Who are they, anyway? Hoppers, no doubt.' She turned up her nose.

'Yes, hoppers, but I knew many of them.'

'Gypsies and those filthy Londoners and Irish. Well, I shall go on, but I expect you to be on your way to the brewery as soon as you have dressed.' She turned her horse towards the Hadlow road and cantered off, leaving Richard speechless with rage.

Ignoring Clarissa's demands, Richard first went to the inn to see if any more bodies had been found, then he walked to the bridge. The lane was congested with people, donkeys, horses and trailers. Most of them were gypsies, as word had quickly spread throughout Kent, and all the tribes had come to mourn their kinfolk, many of them from other shires. His heart sank when he encountered a cart in which four bodies lay. He asked the carrier who they were.

'Don't know, but you can look and see if you know dem,' he said.

'No need,' said a man, walking beside the cart. Richard recognised the gypsy who had asked the waggoner if he could ride on the hind horse. 'One young lady is Irish, I'm told. The other three are relatives of mine, Comfort Leatherland and her niece

Centine and James Manser a distant cousin.' He shut his eyes and opened them slowly. "They are all my people.'

'Centine, not little Centine,' Richard cried. He thought of her tiny, wet hand in his and her shouting goodbye in Roma. 'Oh, how can you stand it?'

'Do you know her?'

'I know her – I know them all. I was with them picking hops the year before last. I was so – so…' He could not find words. 'Did you know that Fanny is with Mr Cox?'

'No, not where she was, but I knew she had been rescued. I will go and see her when I have taken these bodies to the inn, and I have found a Rom to stand by them.'

'I think Fanny will be called for the inquest this afternoon. It's to be held at the Bell. Look after her.' Richard hurried away, too upset to speak any more, but marvelling at the calm of the man whose whole life, like Fanny's, would never recover.

The people he saw at the bridge and along the banks disgusted him. Many of them were ghoulish onlookers who hampered the genuine rescuers by getting in the way and churning up the meadowland where the water had spread. Richard wondered why no boat was sent to help the rescue. What had happened to the manhandled barges that travelled daily to or from Maidstone? Had someone stopped them? Was nobody in authority concerned? Did they think, like Clarissa, that they were persons of no consequence? Perhaps answers would be given at the inquest that afternoon.

Inquest Saturday afternoon, 22 October, 1853

The small room was crowded. William Cox sat dejectedly, his head drooping, his eyes closing and opening slowly, and he appeared as if he had had no sleep, which probably was the case. Beside him sat Fanny Leatherland, her eyes swollen and red. Several other men were there, as well as those making up the jury. Mr Gorham, the solicitor to the Medway Navigation Company and a Mr Hallowes, one of the company managers, sat to one side.

The twelve men, mainly local tenant farmers, were sworn in.

'Now, gentlemen', the Coroner, Mr Dudlow, said, 'you are gathered here to decide if the death of these persons was occasioned by the gross negligence or carelessness of any party that would constitute manslaughter. You must also decide from the evidence whether such gross negligence or carelessness had, in this case, caused so fearful a catastrophe. On the other hand, were the deaths solely the result of an accident; you must frame your verdict accordingly.'

Mr Dudlow now directed that they go to view the bodies, and afterwards they would go to the scene.

'This is a sorry state of affairs,' John Larking said, as they walked across the yard to the stable that was serving as a temporary morgue.

'It is indeed,' said a fellow farmer, named Giles Edwards. 'I never thought to be in such a position as this in my life.'

'How many still missing?' another farmer asked John Eldon.

'Well over twenty, the exact figure isn't known for sure. Friends and relatives are still out there, prodding the banks, shouting names, crying. 'Tis a pitiful sight. We'll see them when we go there.'

'I hear that word has spread and all the gypsy tribes are coming from the shires. Is that true?'

'Yes, I believe so,' the landlord said. 'Mr Cox has let them camp on his land wherever they can. He is quite distraught.'

'Someone told me,' said William Kipping, 'that the gypsies are after the waggoner, 'cause they consider it's his fault.'

'Yes, I heard that. But he's in the inn at the present time, in case he's called as a witness.'

They reached the stable. The six were laid forth - two women's bodies had been in the stable since Friday morning. Four bodies had been carried in not an hour before the inquest had started, the saddest sight being a little girl of around four years of age. The men solemnly filed past. The names of the deceased were written on cardboard and attached to the rough brown blankets covering them, Centine Hern; Charlotte Leatherland; Comfort Leatherland; Catherine Roach; Norah Donovan; James Manser. A gypsy stood close by, his head bowed, a candle burning beside him.

Saturday afternoon

Charles Everest tied his horse to a branch of a tree about a hundred yards from the bridge. He could get no nearer for the masses. Notebook and pencil in hand, he had to force his way towards the wooden bridge. He had learned about the accident from his editor who had received a telegraph message about some hop-pickers falling in the Medway near Tunbridge.

'Ride over there, Charles, and see what it's all about,' he said. 'I've been told they are mostly gypsies and Irish. There'll be some background story you can find, I'm sure. I've sent Siddall to cover the inquest.'

But never in all his ten years as a reporter had he witnessed such a scene of utter misery and anguish. Men and women were running along the sides of the river shouting, calling names, scrabbling dangerously on hands and knees near the water's edge. Others were knee deep, prodding to find where the river bank started. The whirling pools were being poked with poles to see if any bodies were trapped there. Mothers with young children holding their hands or skirts, were standing mute with grief. Horses and donkeys that had brought relatives to the scene were chomping on grass, unconcerned at the scenes around them.

Charles pushed a path to study the shattered side of the bridge where the waggon had crashed into it, then he slid down to the mud-churned water's edge. The river roared past; the milling crowd, now numbering hundreds, shouted above the noise. He surveyed the broken fencing from below. It was undoubtedly rotten and he could see how the accident could have happened on that narrow bridge. Maintenance was sadly lacking. Throngs of gypsies stood in clusters, the women crying silently, the men distraught - many angry.

He asked a young man if he knew how many people had been saved, and was told it was estimated eleven, and thirty had perished, many of them gypsies from the same family.

'Did you know them?' Charles asked, reaching into his pocket for his pencil and opening his notebook.

'I knew all of them by sight, and some well.'

'When did you know about the accident?'

'About half an hour after it happened, maybe less. I stayed until the early hours of yesterday morning, when two bodies were found. Four more were discovered sometime during last night or early this morning.'

'May I ask your name?'

'Richard Wakefield.'

'Are you from these parts?'

'I live here now, but I originally come from the outskirts of London.'

'Thank you, Mr Wakefield. I'll leave you to your sorrowful task.'

Charles returned to his horse and wrote in his book while the scenes were fresh in his mind -

'I found groups of bereaved friends and relatives standing about in mute despair - others with animated gesticulations were describing the terrible catastrophe - some with long poles were probing the eddies and backwaters of the river for the bodies of those that were lost - it was pointed out to me that one gypsy woman had lost father and mother and infant brother - one man had lost fourteen relatives - another, a man whose face and mien were the personification of grief itself, threw a piece of wood to direct the men with poles to the spot where he had last caught a glimpse of his drowning wife.

Back at the inquest, the first witness was called.

'Please state your name and occupation.'

'My name is Dennis Collins,' the man said, 'and I'm a labourer.'

'Where do you live?'

'In Rosemary Lane. That's in London, Sir, near Tower Hill.'

'And what relationship do you have to any of the deceased you've seen?'

'Well, Sir, they was me friends. We'd all been hop-picking together at Thompson's Farm.' He nodded in the direction of William Cox. 'Oh, yes, Sir. Sure and we come every year.'

'Tell me about your friends.'

'Norah Donovan was a single woman, I think about thirty. We were picking day afore yesterday for Mr Cox. When it was time to go home we went in a waggon.'

'Do you usually go home in a waggon?'

'Oh, no sir, we usually walk. But Mr Cox, he said he would provide a waggon because he had been told the water was so high it would be up to our waists as we got close to the river. It's been raining for several days, you know, Sir.'

There were some smiles as the Coroner said, 'Yes, Collins, we had noticed this. Go on.'

'The water was on the road, on both sides of the river, but not as high as the crown of the bridge.'

'How deep would you say the water was?' the foreman, Thomas Kibble, enquired.

'I'd say from a foot and a half to two feet, Sir. When we got on the bridge I heard a crack, but there were so many people in the waggon, I could not see what had happened. We were more than halfway over the bridge. Directly I heard this crack I found meself falling into the water. There were a great many others thrown in as well as meself.' Collins hands wound round each other. 'Then, Sir – then....'

'Take your time.'

'Then, Sir, I found some wood beside me in the water, a piece of the bridge, and I caught hold of it but I could not hold on for long as the water was flowing fast and pulling me down the river - and one of the pole pullers saved me.'

'And what was happening about you.'

'I could hear some hallooing under the bridge. It was the left hand side of the bridge going towards Tudely that gave way.'

'Did you know whether the waggon went over into the water?'

'I didn't know at the time, but I saw and heard a good many others round about in the water. But it was dark, Sir, or nearly so at the time.'

'Thank you Mr Collins.'

The next witness was Fanny Leatherland. She had been sobbing uncontrollably since their return from the stable and the Coroner tried to soothe her, and let her compose herself before asking her any questions. They learned that she was from Notting Hill in London and she was single.

'Did you recognise any of the deceased?'

'Yes, my mother Charlotte and my sister Comfort. My father is drowned but they have not yet found his body.' Fanny wept and the men shifted uncomfortably in their seats moved by her distress, even though she was a gypsy.

'How old are your mother and sister?'

'My mother is 54 and my sister 24. She is single like myself.'

'How many do you think were in the waggon?'

'I've no idea how many, but I think about forty. There are six more of my closest family not yet found.' Gasps were heard as she went on, 'My father, three sisters, the husband of one of those sisters and their baby - and others.' Still more sobs came from Fanny.

Mr Dudlow, who had doubtless presided over many an inquest of a distressing nature, found it difficult to find words to continue. After an uncomfortable silence he said, 'When you are ready Miss Leatherland, we do need to move on. Can you tell the jury how you think the accident happened?'

Fanny blew her nose and tried to control her emotions. However, as she looked up at the Coroner, her shoulders still rose and fell with stifled sobs.

'I didn't see exactly. The waggon went over all at once. We just had time to say - to say "Oh Lord" and we found ourselves in the water.'

'What about the waggoner?'

'I knew him, but not his name.'

'Was he drunk or incapable of handling a waggon?'

'No, he was quite sober at the time I am sure.'

'Go on.'

'The waggoner rode on the fore horse. The water was out over the road on this side – the Golden Green side. The water was over the horses' knees and up to the foot of the bridge. The driver could not walk on this side because of the water so that's why he was riding.' Fanny sniffed and wiped her eyes. 'When we got over the other side of the bridge the hind horse slipped and nearly fell down. Benjamin, a kinsman of mine, was on this horse and tried to pull his head round but before he could, the wheel came into contact with the railing of the bridge and it broke and the waggon tipped into the water.'

'How did you escape?' the foreman asked.

'The whole of the persons in the waggon were thrown into the river and they came tumbling over me like hailstones. I took hold of the waggon first then the harness of the hind horse, which reared up, and the waggoner hearing me cry called out to Mr Cox's pole puller who dragged me out. I could see how the accident happened perfectly well.'

'Have you identified any other of the deceased brought in this morning?'

'Yes. James Manser is my cousin's brother-in-law. Centline Hern is my sister's little girl.'

Have you often crossed this bridge?'

'Oh, yes, many times. The last time was on Wednesday when the same man drove us. He was very careful and they was the same gris – I mean horses.'

'Thank you Miss Leatherland. You have been most helpful. May I say on behalf of all of us here how deeply sorry we are at the loss of so many of your family.'

There were murmurs of agreement from everyone in the room as Fanny sat down on a chair behind the jurors.

In one corner of the room a reporter sat scribbling in his notebook.

William Clearly was the next witness. He told the jurors that he was from county Cork but lived in Woolwich, in London and that he was a labourer.

'I know all the deceased whose bodies I've seen, Sir, because we've all been hopping together for years. Kitty Roach is – was – a single woman about twenty-two I believe, Sir.'

'Could you explain the situation how you saw it, Mr Clearly?'

'Well, Sir, we had left work about six o'clock to go to our homes.' He frowned. 'Yes, it was about six o'clock because day and night had hardly parted. We had to go over the bridge and there was a great deal of water out in the road. It was up above the belly of the horses in the deepest part. The man in charge of the waggon had to ride. He got up on the front horse. Because the waggon was so full, a man, a gypsy I think, had asked the waggoner if he could ride upon the hind horse before we left.'

'When we got over the bridge, someone touched the hind horse, which was a young grey and the horse sprung forward a little. I think the rider didn't look after him properly and the horses was kept too close to the corner and went against the railing. Everyone except three men fell into the water. These three men jumped out before they got to the bridge.'

'What do you mean by 'before they got to the bridge'?' Do you mean while still in the road?'

'No I means they jumped when they were at the top of the bridge, when the waggon tipped. The horse was struck slightly just as they were getting to the top of the bridge. When they got to the top, we thought everything was all right. The hind horse did not slip or stumble but he hung back going down on the other side of the bridge. The waggon didn't overpower the horses. I believe it was the hind wheel that struck the fence, and the waggon went over immediately. One of the shafts was broken and I heard the wheel crash against the fence. I was sitting at the front, on the off side and I couldn't see the wheels on the other side.'

'Have you been over this bridge before, Mr Clearly?'

'Oh yes, Sir, many times.'

'Do you know the waggoner?'

'Yes, though I don't know his name. He went very carefully.'

'Then what happened?'

'I was thrown into the water, but I managed to catch hold of the waggon and that saved me. The water was running very strong and the banks were overflowed so that they couldn't be seen.'

The next witness was John Lawrence, Mr Cox's farm bailiff and hop-measurer. He concurred with the time the hoppers left. He said the waggoner was John Waghorne. 'He had already taken one party of hoppers home to Tudely,' he informed them, 'and came back for the others. I was in the back part of the waggon on the off side. As we neared the bridge, the water was so deep that John had to get upon the front horse. Benjamin Hern, I believe that's his name, was already on the rear horse for the same reason.'

'Were the horses restive at all?' asked the Coroner.

'No, they went very steadily. When we got just over the crown of the bridge the hind horse made a stumble - I heard the ringing of the shoe. The waggon swerved when the horse stumbled and the near hind wheel began to go down and appeared to overpower the horse. John heard the horse struggle and looked back and tried to guide the horse to the off side of the road. I heard him call hoot, hoot, but the wheel appeared to me to sink between the timber of the bridge and the earth.'

'What did you think about the state of the bridge?' asked Mr Maplesden, a juror.

'I have often noticed the holes between the timbers and the earth. I could put my foot in them.' He made to demonstrate with his boot. 'I didn't hear a crash but as the waggon sunk down, the fence was throw out by the wheel, that made it tip over and threw the people in the front over the heads of the others.'

He told the jurors that the waggoner was quite sober. He was a careful steady man and that the bridge, which was very narrow, had been in a very bad state for a long time. The timbers appeared to be rotten; the boards were parting from the earth. The fence did not appear to be faulty but the top of the boards leaned over towards the river, and he had often spoken about it to others.

'Was any complaint made to anybody in authority?'

'Not to my knowledge, Sir.'

'Were you thrown into the water?'

'No, I managed to jump out. The current was very strong and all those thrown into the river were immediately swept away.'

'Thank you Mr Lawrence.'

Henry Knight, a labourer from Camberwell, said that at the time of the accident he was at the front. 'I was speaking to my daughter Selina when the fence broke - I tried to grasp her - I tried to grasp her hand, but....' He pressed his knuckles to his mouth and with his other hand searched in his pocket for something to wipe away his tears. All the men in the room had their heads bowed, overwhelmed by the evidence they were hearing, and trying, unsuccessfully, to comprehend the experience and heartbreak of each witness they heard.

The Coroner waited.

'.... I tried to grasp her hand, but I couldn't - I couldn't - because we were all so tightly packed. I was thrown down between the horse and the fence. In my opinion, the horses were not sufficiently in the middle of the road , it being so narrow, so the wheel struck the fence. That's my impression, Sir.'

'Do you think the bridge was in a poor state?'

'Yes, Sir, for the last four or five years it has been broken away and decayed. I think it was unsafe to go over with a heavy load, let alone with such a lot of poor creatures as we had.'

'Thank you, Mr Knight, that will be all.'

The inquest continued with the testimony of Benjamin Hern.

'I was riding on the hind horse. As we were going over the bridge and down the other side, the hind horse tripped against one of the irons on the bridge. Before I could recover myself, the ground gave way and the waggon went over, the hind part going first.'

'Did the wheel touch the fence?'

'I couldn't say. We were riding as near the middle as we could and going very steady but the bridge is not wide, I think only nine feet.'

'Do you think the waggoner could have prevented the accident?'

'No, Sir, he couldn't possibly have done so. I think the fault was in the bridge. It wasn't strong enough to bear that load. The part of the road next to the fence gave way before the wheel touched the fence at all.'

'I understand that many of your family are drowned or missing.'

'Yes, Sir. The Leatherlands, Taylors and Herns are all related to me and James Manser is my wife's brother. Thomas Taylor is my uncle. All but four are still missing.'

The coroner asked the assembled company if anyone that they knew about had complained to the Medway Navigation Company about the state of the bridge. James Hughes, one of the jurors said that the dilapidated state of the bridge had been very perceptible for some time, but he did not know that any formal complaint had been made.

Mr Gorham whispered something to Mr Hallowes. The reporter stopped writing and leaned forward to study the faces of the two men.

'I have not called John Waghorne,' Mr Dudlow informed them, 'because I didn't know whether the evidence would have inculpated him but, as it is, there doesn't seem to be anything like gross neglect or culpable negligence on the part of the waggoner. I, therefore, propose to call him.'

An ashen-faced John Waghorne came into the room and sat facing the coroner.

He began. 'Mr Cox asked me if I would take the hoppers home because of the state of the roads. I took one lot home, mostly home dwellers, and came back for the rest. I was in charge of the waggon and the two horses. I don't know how many there were in the waggon – thirty-five to forty I would have thought. As we neared the bridge, the water was so deep that I decided to get up on the front horse, which I had been leading. When we were nearly over, the hind horse stumbled by kicking up against one of the irons that cross the bridge. The man behind me on the horse tried to recover him and did so, but the hind wheel sank into the ground before the front wheel touched the fence. The waggon fell over upon the side fence breaking it right through. Nearly all the people were thrown into the river, but one or two managed to jump out.

'I have gone over the bridge with the waggon to and fro with the hoppers since the water was out, and many times with a much heavier load than I had on Thursday. I have never had to put the skid on. If I had put it on, I could not have got it off again because of the water.'

'Have you heard of complaints about the bridge?'

'Yes, many times, but I don't know that any were made to the proper persons.'

'What would you consider your load was?'

'About two tons, Sir.'

'Did you think the bridge was dangerous?'

'No, Sir, if I did, I wouldn't have gone over it.'

A Mr Johnson, of Mereworth, said he had always gone round through Tunbridge rather than cross the bridge. He had spoken of the state of the bridge to several people, but had never mentioned it to persons in authority, or anyone having to do with it.

The jurors turned to each other frowning, questioning why nothing had been reported to those responsible. Did they think that no one would take any notice of a complaint from an ordinary man? And why was it not inspected?

'That seems to be the whole of the evidence,' Mr Dudlow decreed, 'so I must thank the witnesses for their diligence at what has been for them a most distressing time. However, before you all withdraw, there are some gentlemen present who are connected with the company, and perhaps they would like to make some explanation or to say something to the jury.'

Mr Gorham said that in the last six to seven years, since he had been clerk to the company, there had been no complaint made about the bridge. Had there been any he would have entered it in the minutes of the company and immediate attention would have been paid to it.

The Coroner nodded towards Mr Hallowes, who stood up.

'I have been connected with the Medway Navigation Company for five years and I agree with Mr Gorham that no complaint had been received in that time.'

A juryman enquired whether the bridges were periodically inspected.

'Yes, they are,' Mr Hallowes said. 'I had recently seen the bridge and I noticed the top part leaning over as described by one of the witnesses. I gave orders for its immediate repair.'

Mr Dudlow gave him a look that implied it was like shutting the stable door after the horse had bolted, before he began his summing up.

'It has been shown in evidence,' said the Coroner, 'that although many persons had complained of the insecure state of the bridge, yet they had kept their complaints to themselves, and had not communicated with the company or any of its officers. I must admit that I do not use the bridge myself. My feeling is that when the horses heard their hooves on the resonant wood, they were likely to become restive and frightened. No doubt after this appalling accident, there will be many complaints. We can all see what is actually wanted.

'One of the witnesses, ' he continued, 'when asked whether he had considered the bridge to be in a dangerous state, said that *he* had not considered it so. Now the fence is broken he could easily see how rotten it had become, but at first glance to the superficial eye, the bridge would appear to have been in a perfectly safe condition.

'It must be remembered,' the Coroner went on, 'that there was a weight exceeding two tons resting against that fence and it was from the pressure of so great a weight that the fence gave way. The result has shown that the bridge was not safe, or in a proper state of repair. It should have been attended to before.

'I now terminate these proceedings, gentlemen. I leave you to make your decisions. If you consider there was negligence, you must bring in a verdict of manslaughter. If not, you should bring in a verdict of accidental death.'

Mr Dudlow gathered his papers together, rose from his chair and left the room with Mr William Ware, the Registrar of Births and Deaths for Tunbridge District.

The room remained strangely silent when all but the jurors had left. Then one of them spoke.

'I don't know what to think. There was certainly something wrong with that bridge. My labourers have all mentioned it to me at some time over the years,' said William Duke, who farmed a hundred and sixty five acres nearby. 'And though I don't go that way often, I could see it was in need of some attention.'

'Yes',' said James Waterhouse, who was a tenant farmer at Little Fish Hall, 'we all know it was in a state. But I'm worried. What if we say it's manslaughter.'

'What d'you mean?' Giles Edwards queried. 'Don't you think it was?'

'I do, but if we bring in the wrong verdict, might we - well, might we live to regret it?' James replied.

'Regret it? How?' asked another.

'Well, they all stick together, don't they - those in authority, with money and position?' James replied.

Some of the jurors began to see the way he was thinking.

'You mean the landowners might take it out on us if we bring in a verdict that does not show authority in a favourable light.'

'Just so.'

'But they couldn't just turn us out - who would replace us? Our families have been farming these lands for years and years.'

'Maybe I am being pessimistic but I wouldn't like to take the risk. I think we should bring in the accidental death verdict. I employ thirteen labourers, if I lose my two hundred acres, where will they find employment, not to mention me and my wife and children?' James reiterated.

John Larking of Hadlow Place was appalled. 'We can't do that! No, we can't do that. It was definitely manslaughter, whether I have to pay the consequences or not.'

Some nodded their heads in agreement, others frowned as they thought more deeply on the implication James had put forward.

'Let's all sit down and discuss this calmly,' said Charles Maplesden, at thirty-one, the youngest member of the jury.

So the discussion went on for over an hour until they finally came to a conclusion.

CHAPTER 12

Saturday evening
Richard swiftly collected some cold meat from the pantry and a hunk of bread and walked back to the Bell, eating as he went. He supposed his troublesome cough had developed through being out in the cold and wet with little sleep.

'What's going on now, Mrs Eldon? Has the inquest finished?'

'Yes, some time ago, but the jurors have only just left. I thought they would never go.'

So, what was the verdict?'

'Accidental death.'

'Accidental! Why, it was nothing short of murder. That bridge was in a disgraceful state. Who was supposed to look after it, that's what I'd like to know? Someone told me it had been like that for years. Don't they inspect the bridges? Whose job is it?'

'It belongs to the Medway Navigation Company I believe,' Mrs Eldon told him.

'Well, they ought to be ashamed of themselves. I hope they give some sort of compensation to those poor people.' He took out his watch. 'I'm going back now to see what else I can do.'

'But Richard,' she pleaded. 'John tells me you have had hardly any rest these past two days. You'll be making yourself ill. John said you've got a nasty cough already.'

'I can't help that. I must do something. Do you know how many are still missing?'

'John thought more than twenty.'

Sunday, 23 October
No more bodies were found on Saturday. As usual Richard was up early the next morning, and he walked to Clarissa's to inform her he did not wish to ride.

She greeted him haughtily when she came into the drawing room. 'You did not do as I instructed yesterday. I do not like to be disobeyed. You need to remember your place. You are not indispensable.'

'I realise you are displeased, but I feel it is my duty to - to wait until all the bodies are found.'

'Ride with me first and then, if you must, go back there.'

'I feel too upset to enjoy riding. Next Sunday, perhaps.'

'Will we have the pleasure of your company this lunch time - or is *that* too upsetting?'

'I feel I shall not be pleasant company. Will you make my excuses to your mother, and apologise to her?'

Richard left the room and Susan, who had been outside listening, scuttled to open the front door for him and gave a bob.

'Good morning, Susan. How are you?'

'All right. Ter'ble accident, wasn't it, Sir?'

'Yes, indeed - but as your mistress said, they are only Irish and gypsies, so we have no need to feel concerned.'

'Goodbye, Sir.'

Clarissa came out of the drawing room and cuffed Susan round the ear. 'Get into the kitchen, you lazy slut.'

When Richard arrived at the bridge, five bodies were laid out on the grass covered by coats and rough blankets. The men he had met around their fire a few days ago were standing by.

'Who are they?' he asked Dennis Collins.

'Two of them are gypsies, one is a local man I do not know; the others are ours.'

'Who are the gypsies?' Richard asked. Dennis lifted the coverings from two bodies. 'Lunia and Samuel,' Richard murmured as he peered at their grey, grimed faces which contrasted startlingly with their usual bronzed appearance. Both had gashes to their faces. Their bodies were bloated, the skin stretched and shiny. Richard felt sick.

'And, this is my wife, Ellen, young sir.'

They stared at the swollen face, ashen like the gypsies, hair matted and caught up with silt and weed. He started sobbing and Richard held his arm in comfort. ' I am so sorry,' he said his own tears welling. 'So very sorry. I think this must be one of the most appalling tragedies there has ever been.'

Richard clutched his chest and screwed up his eyes as another bout of coughing hit him. Emotionally he was finding the situation too much to bear. He could not conceive how relatives must be feeling.

'The other one is Jeremiah Murphy.'

'The old chap who was going to buy vegetables from Covent Garden and sell them in the winter?'

Dennis nodded and wiped his eyes.

There was a call, and in the distance they could see two men carrying a body. They shouted, 'Who is it? Who is it?' as they pushed their way through the crowds to see the latest cruel find.

'It's Mary Quinn,' William Clearly told Dennis.

The body of Bridget Flinn was found an hour later.

Richard was coughing as he jumped off the waggon at Thompson's Farm and went to break the news to Fanny.

'How are you?' he asked futilely. 'Was the inquest a terrible ordeal?'

'Yes, but everyone was very kind. Benjamin will look after me. My Taylor relatives from Paddock Wood are here, they are camping on Mr Cox's land. Emily escaped, but her sister, Sarah and her nephew and – and his little boy Thomas. They haven't been found yet, have they? She is very worried.'

'No, Fanny, but Lunia and your father...'

Fanny burst into tears. Richard took her hand and squeezed it. He wanted to hold her close to him but he knew that would not be acceptable behaviour by the gypsies.

'I will report to you all I know. If you think there is anything I can do to help you, please ask. I know you have some of your tribe to comfort you....'

She pushed her thick, black hair from her face, 'Yes, I will ask.' She looked at him closely. 'You look ill. I think you should be in bed, you are too unwell to be abroad. I will ask my mother...' she stared at the ground unable to continue. 'I will make up a potion for you, and take it to the inn.'

'That is very kind of you, Fanny, but I think you are too distressed.'

Thomas Cotter, the curate at St Mary's Church in Hadlow, rode to the inn at Golden Green after morning service. Mr Moneypenny, the vicar, had asked him to conduct the first funerals and consult with the relatives concerning the burials.

'Good morning, Sir,' John Eldon greeted him. 'Let me take your horse.' He led it over to the side barns where all the horses were now stabled.

'Do you want to see the bodies?'

'No, that will not be necessary. Coffins have been made for them, have they not?'

'Yes, Sir. Thirteen coffins of elm are being made and the local carpenters and wheelwright are making more for those not yet recovered.'

'The deceased need to be conveyed to St Mary's. Can I leave that in your hands, Mr Eldon?'

'Of course, Sir. The relatives are inside. Come this way.' John led him through to the room where the inquest had been held.

'This is Benjamin Hern, Sir. He will make any decisions about the six gypsies to be buried. And,' he said, moving on to the next man, 'this gentleman is Dennis Collins and he has been elected as spokesman for the travellers.'

'Thank you, Mr Eldon.'

'Sit down here, Sir.' John indicated a chair behind a table. 'Do you wish me to stay?'

'No, I don't think that will be necessary. They will tell you what arrangements have been made.'

'Very good, Sir. I shall I get my wife to bring you refreshment.'

Monday, 24 October

Richard forced himself up next morning to attend the funeral of the thirteen so far found. While at the funeral, three more of the Irish shed had been found well down the

Medway from the bridge. Thomas Taylor and his mother Sarah were also recovered. He recalled her in the waggon with a little boy about Centine's age on her lap.

Everyone at the funeral urged him to go to his cottage and stay in bed, but he struggled up and walked unsteadily to the farm because he wanted to see Fanny again. However, when he got there he found that she had been spirited away somewhere by Benjamin though, Mr Cox told him, they were still in the area, probably breaking up their encampments.

'They might burn everything,' Mr Cox said, 'I believe they often do.'

In his mind's eye he could see their camp, the bender tents that John Hern had described, mounted on their waggons or on the ground; how they became water-logged in the rainy weather, and how John was going to make a home on wheels for Lunia and his children. But not now. Not ever. Who was there left? None of Fanny's closest family – no parents, no sisters, no nieces. How would she survive this unbelievable catastrophe?

He went on to the bridge, some unknown force drawing him there. As he mingled with the ghoulish crowds he saw two men in the distance.

Dennis Collins, in spite of his grief at the loss of his wife, was attending to any of the Irish that might be found. He shouted, 'Who is it? Who is it? Is it one of ours?'

William Clearly was carrying the lifeless body of a woman, her head hung over his arm and her long, wet hair swayed as he moved

He nodded. ''Tis Catherine Clare.'

Richard pointed to the body carried by another man. 'And this one?' he croaked.

'Her son, but praise be, he's alive – just about,' the stranger replied.

William laid Catherine beside the others and they rushed over to see to the boy.

'Tis a miracle, a miracle, praise be to God.'

'Here, he must be kept warm,' Dennis took off his coat and threw it over the boy lying limp and deathly pale, still in the man's arms.

Richard started coughing. 'Take him - take him - to the nearest cott - cottage, they won't mind.'

The man left carrying the boy, and they asked William how he had come to be alive after nearly three days.

He crossed himself, before saying, 'Sure he seemed to be caught up above the water in some branches but supported by the corpse of his mother.'

'Would he know she was below him?'

'I think not.'

'I hope not,' Richard said as he wiped the sweat from his forehead. 'It would be appalling to think that you had been saved at the expense of your own mother. Let us hope he does survive. His name's Patrick, isn't it?'

'Patrick, yes, Patrick,' Dennis replied. 'You remember Catherine lost her husband two years ago.'

'Yes, they both looked so sad when I saw you last week.' Richard remembered her face and Patrick seemingly unwilling to leave her side. Who would look after him now?

'I wish we had never asked Catherine to join us for hopping, but we thought it was company, that it was for the best.'

'You cannot reproach yourself,' Richard said. He looked towards the bridge, and pointed. 'Look, there's a waggon up there come to take the bodies to the Bell, I expect. Let's move them.' But a bout of coughing prevented him from helping and he was urged, yet again, to go home. They asked some of the stronger men standing around for assistance and the grave, solemn procession stumbled knee deep in mud to the road.

Another funeral was held on Tuesday for these six people   Richard thought he had cried all the tears he could cry, and felt all the emotions he could feel, but when, weak and ill, he saw Patrick Clare sitting on his mother's coffin from Golden Green to St Mary's, he broke down. Every joint ached, and he had to keep resting on his walk home to his cottage. His head throbbed and his cough now caused him intense pain in his chest. Arriving home, he was too weak to get water from the well so, with shaking hands that would hardly obey him, he poured what little cold water there was from the kettle into a cup, took a few sips and carried it upstairs where he fell exhausted on to the bed.

Three more Irish and Fanny's sister Selina and John Hern were found next day.

Grace discovered from Mrs Eldon that Richard had not been at the funerals that Wednesday, and had appeared quite ill at the previous service, and had not waited to see the burial.

'I told him not to keep going out searching in the cold and wet,' she said. 'He is not a robust countryman.'

'Shall I go and see how he is?'

'Yes, I am worried. Go now and when you come back, let me know if I can do anything for him. Oh, and here's something a gypsy left for him.' She reached for a small bottle. 'I don't know whether you should give it to him or not. I don't trust those gypsies, it could poison him.'

'I'll take it and Richard can decide.'

Grace let herself into the cottage. She called Richard's name, but heard no reply. She went to the scullery to see if he were in the garden, then returned and climbed the stairs. Pushing open the door of a bedroom at the front of the cottage, she saw him on his bed, still in outdoor clothes, tossing and flaying his arms, while muttering incoherently.

'Richard. Richard. What is it? How can I help you?'

He continued muttering, seeming to stare but not focussing. He was burning hot.

'Here, drink some of this water.' She picked up the small earthenware cup on the table beside the bed and tried to raise his head, but he moved suddenly which jerked the cup from her hand and some spilled on the bedclothes. She put down the cup and stood, undecided what to do next. Perhaps she should try to cool his face, he was sweating and so hot. She ran downstairs and searched for something to wipe Richard's face. Taking the kettle from its hook, she tipped water on to a cloth and hurried back. Later she tried again to make him drink.

Should she go back to the inn to get help? Ought he to be left alone? Was he ill enough to need a doctor? Grace pushed both her hands into her hair. Was there to be no end to her suffering. She stared at him, as he lay a little calmer, but still sleeping restlessly.

'I can't stand for anything to happen to you. If it did I'd want to die,' she murmured to his flushed face. Though unwilling to leave him, Grace ran back to the inn.

'Mrs Eldon,' she said breathlessly as she went into the kitchen. 'Richard is very ill. I don't know what's wrong with him. Has he got the fever, like my mother?' She remembered how she had looked before she died.

'I knew it, I knew he was doing too much, rushing around in the cold and wet without a coat most of the time, getting little sleep into the bargain. I know he was upset, but....'

'But has he got the fever?' she insisted, her lip trembling. 'Will he die?'

'I don't know, girl. Fetch Mr Eldon and he'll go back with you.'

Seeing the state that Richard was in when they arrived, John Eldon said they should send for a doctor.

'I know Dr Parker,' Grace told him. 'We went to him with Thomas. I will walk into Tunbridge and ask him what to do, and if he will come. I have some money to pay him.'

'I think that would be best. I will take off these clothes,' he said, removing Richard's neckerchief and undoing buttons. 'I need to make him more comfortable. Can you find him a clean nightshirt before you go - and bed clothes? These sheets are damp.'

Dr Parker heard the urgent knock on his front door from his study. The maid went to answer it, but he came into the hall as it was opened.

'Can I see Dr Parker, please.' Grace caught sight of him and gave a bob. 'Doctor, do you remember me? I came with Thomas who was badly burned.'

The doctor nodded and asked her to come into the hall.

'Can you tell me what I should do? My friend Richard is ill, and hot, and flinging himself about and I can't get him to drink and he is so hot, what should I do?' She knew she was gabbling, and repeating herself, but she wanted the doctor to realise how serious it was. She pulled her shawl close about her with shaking hands.

What a pretty girl, the doctor thought, in spite of her distress. He had gathered she was a servant, when she had come previously, but she appeared to have more about her than most in service and spoke without the strong Kent dialect.

'Calm yourself, calm yourself. Come into this room and tell me exactly what is wrong.' He turned to the maid. 'Thank you, Charlotte. I will see to the young lady.' He held the door wide for Grace to precede him.

When Grace had explained, she entreated, 'Please will you come? I have the money, I can pay you.'

'Yes, I will come, but I cannot leave immediately. You go home and keep trying to make him drink. Where does his water come from?'

'There's a well, Sir.'

'How many people use it?'

'I'm not sure, just the three cottages I think, doctor.'

'What is your name?'

'Grace Brandon, Sir.' she said, giving another small curtsey.

'Well Miss Brandon, make sure the water has been boiled before you give it to him. I will ride over as soon as I can. Tell me where I must go.'

Dr Parker dismounted in the lane, and tethered his horse to a nearby tree. Grace, who had been watching at Richard's bedroom window, flew down to let him in. As they mounted the stairs Grace said, 'He has been searching for the bodies in the accident ever since it happened. Day after day, and night times as well. You know about the accident, don't you, Sir? Some of those who were drowned he called his friends.'

The doctor raised his eyebrows, then said, 'It is indeed a dreadful affair. I gather all have not yet been found.'

He opened his bag and took out an instrument to listen to his patient's chest. Grace stood well away and turned from the bed as the doctor pulled down the bedclothes and, raising Richard's nightshirt, he peered all over his body.

'Now what I suggest you do is to continue making him drink as much water as is possible. Make sure it has boiled for at least a minute. Try to keep him cool. I have examined him but I cannot see any rash or anything that makes me think he has cholera or any other contagious disease. However, I do think he has pneumonia and he could die from this, and many people do.'

'He could die!' Grace gasped. 'No, oh, no.' She covered her face with her hands.

'Yes, he could die.' Dr Parker began to replace his instruments in his case. 'I am of the opinion, not held by many doctors I am sorry to say, that it is the poor state of the water that is responsible for much of the illness in and around Tunbridge, and everywhere else come to that. That's why I enquired about his drinking water.' Grace sat on the bedside chair her elbows on her knees, her hands still covering her face. 'In fact,' he went on, shutting up his case with a snap, 'there is a study going on in the town right now. They think the sewers....'

He turned and realised that Grace was not listening. 'You have not had a good time of recent months, have you, Miss Brandon?'

Grace stood up and straightened her back. She reached into her pocket. 'How much do I owe you?'

'Two shillings.'

She gave him two sixpences and a shilling. 'I will see you out, doctor.'

In the main room she said, as she opened the front door, 'How long before we know if he shall - he shall get better? Is there anything else I can do?'

'You should start to see an improvement in two to three days. Do as I told you, drinks and keep bathing his face. If he has a man friend, perhaps he could wash him. I do not think that is something you should be doing.'

She gave him a wan smile. 'I shall do as you say, Sir. Thank you, Sir.' She curtsied. 'Can I come and fetch you again if I am worried?'

'Of course.' He put on his top hat, and she watched as he mounted his horse and rode back to Tunbridge.

That evening, John Eldon came to see the position and, at Grace's request, washed Richard and stayed a while so Grace could catch up on some sleep.

Richard lay comatose for several days, rousing occasionally to mutter a few unintelligible words. Grace stayed at his house night and day, not caring if Mrs Eldon was upset or not. Richard was her only concern; he must not die and if doing what the doctor said prevented it, then she would stay however long it took.

CHAPTER 13

'Grace, what are you doing here?' Richard's voice was faint and shaky, his eyes heavy lidded. He tried to raise himself in the bed, but fell back.

She jumped up from her chair and cried, 'Oh, Richard, you're back., you're back. I've been so worried. Here, drink this water.' She struggled to get him sitting up, making them both breathless.

He took a long draught. 'Have I been in bed for long? I remember going to bed after the funeral.'

'Four days. Dr Parker came to see you. You have pneumonia.'

'Four days? No it can't be. Have I really?'

'That's what the doctor said. He said you were to have lots and lots of water that had been boiled, but I've had difficulty making you drink. Dr Parker thinks the water is bad in the town, and there is something going on in Tunbridge, something to do with the sewers.' She paused. 'He said you could die.'

Richard smiled at her. 'Not yet. Have you called in to see how I was?'

'No, I have been here all the time.'

'All the time! Four days?'

She nodded. 'Ever since I knew you were ill.'

'Has Miss White been told, has she been here?'

'I think Mrs Eldon told Susan, but I have not seen Miss White.'

'I don't know what to say.'

'Here, drink some more. Lots and lots, that's what the doctor said. I expect you are hungry.'

'Yes, I feel ravenous.' He drank more water at Grace's insistence, and collapsed on to his pillow at this exertion.

When Richard first became ill, there remained five people to be found. Alice Leatherland was the first and she was committed two days later. The two adults still missing were Margaret King and Catherine Donohue and the three children - Henry Knight's daughter, Selina, little Thomas Taylor and Centine Hern's baby sister.

When Grace told him that three more bodies had been found, Richard said he was going to the funerals, but Grace absolutely forbade him to move out of the cottage, saying she would lock him in if necessary.

'You're not strong enough yet. I will go for you.'

'You know, this reminds me of when I first knew you. So determined.'

'Why are you not riding with Richard this morning? I am sorry not to see him, such a charming young man.' Mrs White asked. Clarissa was standing in the hall adjusting her riding habit. 'Did you say he was not well?'

'So I was told. Susan brought me a note from Mrs Eldon at the Bell. You would have thought he could have told me himself.'

'How could he if he were ill?'

'It couldn't be that bad. I expect he caught a cold dashing around looking for those gypsies. Stupid man. Anyway, he did send a message in the end. Said he had been in bed for four days.'

'I expect you miss him at the brewery.'

'Oh, we've managed. Mark Littlejohn is just as efficient as Richard. In fact, I don't think we have felt his loss at all.'

'Do you not think you ought to visit him? How long has he been away?'

'Well over a week.'

'And you have not bothered to discover how he is? He could be dead.'

She gave a twisted smile. 'I think I would have heard if he had died.'

'What about all he did to pull that failing brewery into one that is now in much better standing. Have you no gratitude?'

'I run a business, not a charity, anyway he is well paid - very well paid.' She thought of her desperate need for Richard to help her. 'Unfortunately he was getting above himself. Defying me when I gave him specific instructions.'

'You are a heartless woman.'

Richard was reading the Maidstone Gazette. 'Well,' he said to Grace who was clearing out the grate. 'I never thought anyone would write such a thing - and him a clergyman.'

Grace came and looked over his shoulder. 'What's wrong?'

'It's a tract from a Reverend R Shindler who sees fit to find a moral for the disaster. Listen to this.'

"There is something mysterious about the incident, for those thirty persons were all gypsies or Irish and, not only had a party of home dwellers been conveyed across the bridge in safety a short time before, but certain trivial circumstances had prevented several residents uniting with the party that met so melancholy an end.

"Someone may say this fact explains all, they were notorious sinners I doubt not, and God has punished them for their sins with a dreadfully sudden death.'

'But then he goes on to say, feeling guilty I suspect.'

"I suppose that, in fact, the doomed party may have been no worse than some of the home dwellers."

'They've found another two bodies, Richard,' Grace informed him next day. She no longer stayed at the cottage because Richard was strong enough to be up and she only came in to bring him provisions and prepare the occasional meal.

'Who are they?'

'I don't know their names, but they are Irish. The funeral is tomorrow.'

'I must go.'

'I wish you wouldn't.'

'I am all right now.'

'But it's cold and there's a strong wind. Please don't go.'

Richard was going to argue, but he could see how distressed she was. He owed her so much. No loving wife could have been more considerate and unselfish.

'Very well, Grace.' He saw her give a sigh of relief. 'There are not many bodies to be found now I should think. I have lost count.'

'I heard Mr Eldon say there was only a baby.'

'If it's a baby, it must be John and Lunia's. I reckon Mr Eldon was right, the tiny body is probably caught up in reeds and might never be found.' Richard swallowed, and just prevented himself from bursting into tears, bringing home to him just how frail he was mentally as well as physically.

A week later Richard told Grace he was going to work the following Monday.

She frowned. 'Are you sure you are well enough?'

'I have been for a little walk for the last three mornings. Tomorrow I shall walk to Clarissa's and tell her I'm coming back. I wonder she has not been to see me.'

'It's still cold. Wrap up warm and go by the Bell so that you can rest there on the way in case you get tired.'

'Yes, Grace, I shall do everything you say.'

'I don't want you to get ill again, that's all,' she said, seriously. She remembered what the doctor had said about dying of pneumonia.

'I shall be very, very careful, I promise - and I think I can manage to get all my own meals from now on. You have been so kind. I would like you to do my shopping for me, as usual, if you will. You know, I rather fancy some oysters. Can you get some next time you are at Tunbridge market?

Grace was disappointed that he no longer wanted her, but on the other hand, Mrs Eldon was getting impatient about the amount of time she was away from the inn. Last weekend there had been two guests and, Mrs Eldon had informed her, she was badly needed.

Richard managed to walk the mile and a half to Clarissa's, but when he arrived he found that she had not come back from her Saturday morning at the brewery.

'Shall I tell Mrs White you are here?' Susan asked.

Richard desperately wanted to sit down, but he did not want to bother Clarissa's mother. However, when Mrs White came out of the drawing room, his prayer was answered.

'Richard, how lovely to see you. I have so missed you.' She turned to Susan. 'Get us some cakes and tea, Susan.' The maid shut the front door and disappeared into the back of the house.

'Come and sit down. Clarissa said you have been ill.'

'Yes, I have had pneumonia.'

'Dear me. You look so very thin and pale.'

'I am tired after my walk. Perhaps, as Grace said, I think I am fitter than I am.'

'Ah, Grace, I have heard her mentioned. Who is she?' This was obviously the young woman whose presence had worried her daughter.

'When I first came to Golden Green two years ago, Grace had recently lost her mother to the fever, and her father had left. John Eldon and his wife took her in. But I liked her. In spite of her background, she had a spark about her. I taught her to read, you know. She is intelligent, but girls in her position have no chance of bettering themselves. When I was ill, she stayed with me for three days and nights until I came out of a coma.'

'A little unconventional, don't you think?'

'No one else was bothered or could spare the time.' Mrs White nodded, realising his implication. 'The reason I have come is to say I intend to return to the brewery the day after tomorrow. Will you inform Clarissa?'

'Yes, of course. Shall you be riding or having a meal with us tomorrow?'

'I'm not sure if I'm ready for riding, but I would love to lunch with you, thank you.'

Susan came into the room and put the tray on a small mahogany table. 'Shall I pour, Mrs White,' she said, hoping to hear some conversation of interest.

'No thank you. I'll do it.'

While taking tea, Clarissa returned.

'Why, Richard, how pleasant to see you at last. You have been ill you told me.'

'Richard has had pneumonia and was in a coma for several days', Mrs White informed her.

'Really, that bad. That's what comes of mixing with all those gypsies and other vagabonds.' She turned to her mother. 'I am going to change, Mother. I shall join you in fifteen minutes.'

Richard sighed heavily. 'I seem not to be in favour. I went hop-picking with some of those gypsies two years ago,' he continued, 'and do not regard them as others do. They were kind to me. Just because they live a roving life, it doesn't mean they are all terrible people. I cannot see that they are any different from anyone else. No one deserves to have such misfortune thrust upon them. Do you know that one young gypsy girl has lost her mother, father, four sisters, two nieces and brother-in-law. In addition, some other relatives of hers were also drowned. How can anyone survive that, whatever class they belong to?'

Mrs White could see how distressed he was, and reached out a hand to touch his.

Clarissa returned and her mother said, 'Shall I get Susan to make you fresh tea, dear.'

Clarissa nodded and her mother reached for the bell pull.

'Well, Richard, when are you intending to return?'

'On Monday.'

'Good.'

'Is there anything outstanding that I shall have to attend to immediately? I don't think I have to go to Cranbrook Hop Market yet, do I?'

'I don't know. Mark will tell you. He has been a *great* asset in your absence.'

He felt overwhelmingly dispirited. It was obvious that Clarissa was unconcerned about him or his welfare. He sat silently until Mrs White said, as she held out a plate of cakes for him to choose, 'Shall you be riding tomorrow?'

Clarissa glared at her mother. 'It is not for you to ask.'

Richard said, 'How is Chanticleer?'

'Jakes has been riding him most days. Did you miss him?'

'Jakes or the horse?' Richard asked, ingenuously, unable to resist a little levity to relieve his gloom.

Mrs White giggled.

'The horse, of course. Don't play games with me.'

His voice serious, he said, 'For several days I was not in a position to miss anything, having been in another world. However, it is obvious my loss was not felt.' He stood up, returning his cup to the tray. 'I'll bid you farewell, Mrs White.' He held out his hand. 'Thank you so much for the tea and your invitation to luncheon tomorrow, and your past hospitality. I am sorry, but I shall have to decline as I sense my presence will be an embarrassment.'

Richard left the room without acknowledging Clarissa. It was against his principles to be so rude, but he could not believe any person could behave so insensitively and in such an uncaring manner.

Apart from preparing himself light meals, Richard sat in his chair all the rest of that day. He was exhausted from his walk to and from the Whites' house. Grace had been and the cottage sparkled. The pantry was stocked, the bed made and his clothes tidied. She offered to do his washing for him, but he said it could go to the laundress in the village, as usual.

He stretched out his legs and put his hands behind his head. He needed to take stock, as he had when he first arrived in Golden Green and had bought the cottage. Now his illness had put fresh thoughts into his mind.

What was important in his life? *Who* was important? Should he move to another part of the country and explore that? His dear brother would be behind him, willing him to broaden his horizons. He had money, was unlikely to be out of work for any length of time because he had experience in rescuing a business. Anyway, he could live off his savings for a while if need be. Where would he go if he did choose another part of the country? He was not sure he even wanted to leave the south of England.

However, he had no desire to return to the brewery and neither did Clarissa want him there, it appeared. Life would be too fraught and he would be unable to cope the way he felt at the moment. So much for loyalty. But this was commerce and loyalty was not recognised or rewarded. He had done as he had been asked to the best of his ability and had been rewarded well for it. Mark Littlejohn was efficient and could take his place even though he might struggle for a time. Another clerk could be found for keeping the books. He had self-satisfaction from what he had achieved there, whether Clarissa acknowledged it or not.

He riddled the fire, lifted the grating and put in a fresh apple log and some coal from the brass scuttle. Even this small task tired him and he fell back in his chair.

And there was Grace. He did not want to leave her either. Whereas he had once thought of her as a pretty, bright child, he now thought of her as a beautiful young woman. But it was not only her beauty that was attracting him, it was her - what phrase could he use - devotion during his illness. She did not have to sit with him hour after hour. In fact, it could have had an adverse effect on her character. Her feelings were that he was not to be left alone, and she was not going to let that happen, whatever might be thought of her by Mrs Eldon or anyone else in the village.

He had reached another crossroads in his life and big decisions had to be made. He would wait until he had been back at the brewery for a week or two to see the lie of the land. If it was as he thought it might be, he would give in his notice.

John was painting the new window frames on the front of the inn. It was a dull November day, though cold. He wiped his hands on a cloth and shook Richard's, greeting him cordially. 'You have lost a great deal of weight I see You look like one of the hop poles.'

Richard laughed. 'Yes, Grace is trying to fatten me up. Is your wife about? I would like to speak to you both.'

They went through the bar and tap room and across the passage to the kitchen. Grace was peeling vegetables and beamed at him. Jane Eldon was cutting up meat to put in a basin. On a marble slab beside her was a pastry crust waiting to be put on the meat.

'Why Richard, how good to see you. How thin you are!' she exclaimed.

'If anyone else says that, I shall think I have faded away completely! When you do not eat for several days, it is inevitable.'

'You were never very fat to begin with, was he Grace?' Jane said.

'Um, do you think, um - can you spare a few minutes' He glanced at John and Jane, ignoring Grace.

'Of course. Are you all right, Grace? Shall we go up to the sitting room?'

Grace stared after them. What could he be wanting to say that she could not hear? Perhaps he was going away and her eyes filled at the thought of not seeing him again. Surely he would tell her.

'Sit down, you look tired,' John said, indicating a sofa by the window.

'I cannot walk very far now without resting. I'm the old softie that Grace used to call me.'

'I think not,' they both chorused.

'I just wanted to thank you for letting Grace care for me. I know it must have inconvenienced you.'

'She didn't give us much choice,' Jane said brusquely. 'She just disappeared, got a doctor at John's suggestion, and we never saw her again till you came to, so to speak.'

'Nevertheless, you could have made life unpleasant for her, given her notice and told her to look elsewhere for a job.'

'We might have done that if it had not been you she was caring for,' Jane Eldon said. John's glance suggested that he would have let Grace help, whoever it was.

'I expect I owe you money for the doctor.'

'No, Grace paid him and I don't know how much he asked for.'

'How kind she has been, so very kind - and you also. I feel so indebted to you since I first came here. What with the tragic drowning and my illness, I feel very emotional.' They stared at him as he endeavoured to get himself under control. 'You see, I am not fully recovered, as Grace has been impressing upon me. I'm not sure how I shall manage on Monday when I return to the brewery.'

'You are going back so soon?' John exclaimed.

'I thought I ought to. Thank you once again for all you have done for me. I shall pay Grace on my way out. Now, I need to discuss with you, and get your opinion on something very important that I intend to do in a few months' time. But I urge you to keep it to yourselves.'

Leaving the Eldon's sitting room, he went down the creaking stairs which reminded him of his first stay there. What a great deal had happened since then.

In the kitchen he said to Grace, 'How much do I owe you?'

Puzzled, she said, 'But you have already paid, don't you remember?'

'No, for the doctor's visit, I mean.'

'Oh, that. I don't want any money?'

'But I insist. You cannot afford to pay for my debts.'

'I can afford what I want to afford.' She tossed her head. 'I shall not take your money.'

The emotions of the day, not to mention his exertions, were taking their toll and he felt too weary to argue. He could always make it up in some other way.

'Very well. Thank you very much - for everything. Have you been to the cottage today?'

'Yes, I have tidied up and bought you fresh provisions which are in the cupboard in the pantry. I have also put clean bedclothes on your bed.'

'What can I say?' He went over to give her a hug and kissed the top of her head.

She wished he was kissing her passionately, and not as a child of whom he was fond. Why did she have to be born so lowly? Apart from elementary reading, she had no skills whatsoever. And being able to read just made her realise what she could have achieved had she not been so poor and ill-educated.

On Sunday, 13 November, Baby Hern was found some way down the river at Yalding, caught in reeds as had been thought probable. She was buried the following day. Richard attended the funeral before going to pick up Chanticleer and ride to Childe's Brewery. He walked past the room where the coopers were busy shaping the wood and banging the bands on the barrels. The familiar thump from the engine room and the strong aroma of the hops gave him a feeling of contentment when he thought of what he had achieved there. His late arrival was noted by Clarissa.

'I have been to the very last funeral - a baby - so you will have no need to worry I shall be late again,' he explained. 'I would like to speak to you alone.'

'Come into my office,' she said. 'What is it, Richard?' She indicated he sit down.

'I wish to leave at the end of the week.'

'You wish to leave! You wish to leave me!'

Much to his surprise she seemed alarmed.

'It is clear that you no longer have any faith in what I can do for you in the future and, as you have said, Mark is very efficient.'

'But *I* want you here.'

'No you don't. What you want is for me to stay for a few more weeks until you and Mark can find out exactly what I do that he shall have to undertake in the future. I have done what you wanted of me, so I shall just become an encumbrance.' Clarissa was lost for words. 'I'm right, aren't I?'

'But I'm not ready for you to go. There's still a lot to be done.'

'I know, but I want a change. My illness, and the consideration given to me by my friends, has shown me what I value. So, I want to leave - as soon as possible.'

'Very well, go if you must,' Her face was flushed and she said furiously, 'you can go right now. I can manage without you, you see if I can't. I gave you a lot of attention - bought the horse, took you to concerts, showed you how those of a better class presented themselves and....'

Richard put up his hand. 'I appreciate all that, but I think you gained as much, if not more from me. Let's just say it was of mutual advantage to us both and leave it at that - and thank you for teaching me to ride a horse, for that I shall always be grateful.' He held out his hand which she ignored.

'Goodbye, Clarissa,' he said, letting his hand drop to his side. 'Do give my regards to your mother. In fact, I shall go and see her when I know you are at the brewery.' He almost added, 'what a pity you do not take after her.'

CHAPTER 14

In 1854 a beautiful memorial was erected in St Mary's churchyard, with the names of the deceased. Richard would stand by the railings after he had been to a morning service and tears would well in his eyes as he read the names that he could recite by heart - and picture most of their faces. He wondered what had happened to the motherless Patrick Clare. It was said that the travellers had taken him.

Medway Navigation had paid more than £60 for the interment and the memorial. In Richard's opinion, the Company seemed to have escaped any major censure on the state of the bridge, even though a rider had been added to the verdict that the bridge should be re-built in stone. As far as he could make out, apart from a few repairs, little else had been done and certainly no compensation had been paid.

'On your birthday....' Richard started, when Grace came to clean.

'On our birthday,' Grace said.

'All right on our birthday next week, I am going to take you out to a concert.'

She grinned broadly. 'Not a concert, Richard, surely not. By the time I get to this promised concert my dress will be above my knees and split down the sides.'

'I shall buy you a new one. This is going to be a very special occasion. You will be seventeen and I will be - very old.'

'No you won't, you'll only be twenty-four.'

'That's very old. I seem to have aged six years in the time I have been here. It must be the air. I've read there's a concert at the Assembly Rooms and I have reserved tickets. It's all right, I have asked Mrs Eldon and she said you can have the time off. I also have something very important to say.'

'How exciting. Why can't you tell me now?'

'Because I don't want to.'

Richard did not buy her a new dress. Grace insisted that they went to Miss Bridger and if she still had some green silk to match, she would have a frill added to the bottom, and perhaps a flower to cover the blood stain.

Grace was as ecstatic over the concert as Richard had been on his first occasion. She particularly enjoyed studying the dresses of the ladies and the handsome soldiers in their red uniforms. Richard was ashamed to admit that he hoped he did not meet anyone he knew. Though Grace was a pretty girl, there was no disguising her humble status, especially if one looked at her hands and feet.

On their way home on the train, she said, 'Oh, Richard. I've never had such a wonderful time as I've had today. And the houses are so grand, and all the carriages, and the dresses.' She looked down at her dress, realising, for the first time, that it was not as fine as she had once imagined. 'I didn't let you down, did I?'

'Of course not. You are beautiful so you do not have to have expensive clothes to show yourself off.'

Grace gave him a wry grin. 'Thank you. I know it isn't true, but thank you for saying it.'

'But you are beautiful, Grace.'

They had to walk from Tunbridge Station to Golden Green, but it seemed no distance as Richard held her hand all the way, much to Grace's delight.

'Come in, Grace, so I can tell you something important.'

'Ah, your mystery.'

'I have not been working for some time now, as you know. However, I can't go on like this. I need to make a big decision about the future.'

Alarmed, she said, 'You're not going away, are you?'

'Yes, emigrating.'

'Emigrating? What does that mean?' He had an expression of excitement in his eyes that she found unsettling.

'It means going abroad - to New Zealand.'

'Abroad? What's abroad and where's New Zealand. Is it in this country?' Grace could not bear the thought that he was leaving to go anywhere, but if it were in this country, she could visit him if she saved up hard enough.

'New Zealand is the other side of the world, past Australia.'

Sobs she could not control, burst from her so suddenly Richard was startled and thought she was going to be sick. He watched aghast as she blindly put out both hands to reach for a chair. She sat down and put her arms on the table and her head on them. Her shoulders shook and she gasped for breath.

Realising how stupid he had been, he rushed over, squatted beside her and put his arm round her still shaking body. 'Grace, Grace, I'm sorry. I should not have put it like I did. I want you to come with me. I want us to get married and travel together.'

She continued crying.

'Did you hear me, Grace? I want to marry you.'

She raised her head slowly and stared at him through her blurred eyes. 'You - you want to *marry me?*'

'Yes, yes.'

'But you're clever and educated and I'm only a servant girl.'

'So, I'm only a clerk. Anyway, what does that matter? In New Zealand we can start a new life. There'll be no class distinction there. We can set up a business of our own. The things we can do are endless. I have enough money saved up for the fare, and when I sell the cottage, there will be money to buy some land. Don't you think it will be wonderful? I have already made some enquiries from the provincial government in

New Zealand.'

Grace continued staring, her hands shaking, still unable to take in all he was saying. Her wildest dreams did not compare with any of this. Richard wanted to marry her, to actually marry her; and then a great adventure on a boat to a new land. She kept shaking her head. 'You are serious, aren't you?'

'Yes, of course. Oh Grace, I'm so insensitive. I didn't mean to upset you like that. I didn't realise that you would miss me so much if I went away.'

'Richard, I have always loved you. Ever since you bought me my shoes and coat I have loved you. I knew you cared about me when you traced me to London, but you never showed any other feelings for me. When you met Miss White, you seemed to go farther and farther away.'

'Grace, you are more worthy of being loved than any Clarissa Whites. She is cold. Remember how she never came to see me when I was ill, but you stayed with me for three days and nights. I knew then I loved you and that we would be happy together. You do think we can be happy together, don't you?'

Still not convinced that this was happening, she said, 'What will Mr and Mrs Eldon say?'

'I mentioned to them a few months ago what I intended, but made them swear they would not say anything.'

'So you decided months ago that you would marry me.'

'Yes.'

'Why didn't you tell me?'

'Because I needed to wait until you were seventeen.'

'That wouldn't stop you telling me.'

'Grace, you're tying me up in knots' He paused, trying to find the right words. 'I wanted to make sure that what I felt for you was not just gratitude for caring for me when I was ill; that I truly loved you, and I do.'

'Oh, Richard, what can I say?'

'Yes, would be a good start.' He kissed her. 'Come on, let's go and tell the Eldons. '

'And all the villagers in the Bell,' Grace said, still not believing what was happening to her. 'And Mrs Eldon will have to find someone else to nag.'

EPILOGUE

Grace and Richard were married in St Mary's, Hadlow in June 1854. Grace insisted that she wear her silk dress but Richard, with the help of Mrs Eldon, prevailed upon her at least to let him have a new one made, in green and in silk if she insisted.

In July 1854 they sailed on 'Blue Jacket' for New Zealand arriving in September. The journey of eighty days, took the southern route, colder, but quicker. Grace had never seen so much money as the thirty pounds he handed over to the shipping agent. Richard had read in the paper of the plight of those who travelled steerage, and when he saw for himself the disgusting food and the crowded and damp conditions, he was doubly thankful that he had paid for a cabin. In true Richard style, he tried to alleviate the lot of the poorer passengers by making petitions to the captain, most of which were met with limited success, as he was reminded that 'We *are* at sea, Sir.'

When they left the boat, they travelled to Nelson where Richard had heard that some German settlers grew hops, and he thought they might try that. They bought some land, but their first experiment was not a success and they grubbed up the hops and planted orchards of apples instead. In six years they had a flourishing business and bought more land on which they grew pears and cherries. They eventually employed twenty men and women, swelling to many more for picking, and Richard insisted that they form a union to which he contributed.

After a further four years they built a grand house that Grace gleefully said surpassed that of Clarissa White's. All their employees and house servants were treated with such consideration, that men and women who had come out on assisted passages knew of the Wakefields' benevolence, and were queuing up to work for them.

The year after they left, Grace wrote to Mr Eldon to say to Susan that if she wished to emigrate (telling him to explain carefully what 'to emigrate' meant and what would be involved) Richard would pay her fare.

Grace gave birth to seven children, Christopher, John, Grace, Henry, Patrick, Fanny and Eliza, and they had so many grandchildren and great grandchildren that Richard said he had lost count. Richard lived to be ninety, but three months after his death, in 1921, Grace died of a broken heart, telling her first born, Christopher, that she no longer wished to live without him and though it would no longer fit her, she was to be buried in the green dress she was married in, which was wrapped in tissue paper in their bedroom.

Mark Littlejohn was cultivated by Clarissa, in the same manner as she had Richard. Unfortunately, Mark had aspirations that she would one day become Mrs Littlejohn. She realised this, but did not disillusion him, not while he would still be of use to her. Nor was it her intention that her business would ever become his. Childe's Brewery continued to flourish and three years after Richard and Grace had emigrated, it was making a decent profit and the money Clarissa had poured in was recovered. The ideas Richard had had for a union were forbidden by Clarissa, but one of the men secretly continued collecting money to give out if any of them was taken ill. Little of the prosperity enjoyed by Clarissa was passed on to her employees.

In 1860 Clarissa broke her neck after falling from her horse while out riding with Mark. Mrs White, now an even richer widow, sold the brewery for a handsome sum and spent her money travelling around Europe, returning for three months in the summer. Mark, now a wiser man, stayed with his new employer.

Susan did take up Richard's offer and she, too, flourished in the New World. Grace, slowly and with difficulty, taught her to read a little, and she married Richard's farm manager and produced five boys.

BIBLIOGRAPHY

Georgian Tonbridge   edited by C W Chalklin, Tonbridge Historical Society

Early Victorian Tonbridge   edited by C W Chalklin, Tonbridge Historical Society

Hopping Down in Kent   by Alan Bignell

Hops and Hop Picking   by Richard Filmer

In the life of a Romany Gypsy   by Manfri Wood

Early Victorian England   edited by GM Young

Human Documents of the Victorian Age   by Royston Pike

A New Dictionary of Kentish Dialect   by Alan Major

Women of Victorian Sussex   by Helena Wojtezak

What it cost the day before yesterday   by Harold Priestley

Preliminary Enquiry into the Sanitary
   Condition of the town of Tunbridge   Alfred L Dickens, Esq

History of Immigration - Settlement in the provinces 1853 to 1870 Te Ara Encyclopedia of New Zealand (internet)

THOSE DROWNED AND THOSE SAVED IN THE
HARTLAKE BRIDGE DISASTER

Drowned (in order of burial)

Charlotte Leatherland	56
Comfort Leatherland	24
Centine Hern	4
Norah Donovan	31
Catherine Roach	21
James Manser	18
Bridget Flinn	20
Lunia Hern	26
Ellen Collins	40
Samuel Leatherland	59
Richard Read	30
Mary Quinn	22
Jeremiah Murphy	50
Ellen Devine	19
Margaret Mahoney	18
Catherine Clare	28
Catherine Presnell	24
Thomas Taylor	38
Sarah Taylor	55
William Elsley	22
Selinda Elsley	25
Ann Howard	49
Selina Leatherland	22
John Hern	28
Alice Leatherland	18
Thomas Taylor	4
Selina Maria Knight	6
Margaret King	20
Catherine Donohue	42
Baby Hern	2
(no name can be found)	

Saved

Benjamin Hern
Fanny Leatherland
Emily Taylor
Nathaniel Taylor
Henry Knight
Dennis Collins
William Clearly
Patrick Clare (fictitious)
John Waghorne
John Lawrence
Will Diplock

Various spellings of names are to be found in newspapers and archives, but I have just stayed with one.

PEOPLE LIVING	FICTITIOUS PEOPLE
AT THE TIME	
(as in 1851 census)	

John and Jane Eldon	Richard Wakefield
Henry Large, shepherd	Grace Brandon
Thomas Willet, shepherd	Brandon, her father
Elias Jones, the carrier	Clarissa White
Leatherlands*	Mrs White
Herns*	Susan
Taylors*	London characters
Irish travellers*	Robert Mills
Mr John Cannel, solicitor	Mr Grieves
(now Warners)	Jakes
Elizabeth Bridger	Jacob Lancing
William Cox	Brewery employees
John Lawrence	Thomas Vanns and family
Will Diplock	Charles Everest/Siddall, reporters
John Waghorne	(though there obviously were
Dr James Parker	real reporters)
Jurors	Mark Littlejohn
Coroner	
Registrar	
Mr Gorham	
Mr Hallowes	
Mr Ware, Registrar	
Curate, Mr Cotter	
Reverend Moneypenny	
Towners	

* Itinerant persons seem not to have
been included in the census.

The monument is still in St Mary's churchyard, minus its railings, and plaques are on the newest bridge at Hartlake. The tragedy is still commemorated, the last time being in 2003. This year, 2008, will be the one hundred and fifty-fifth anniversary.